THE SURVIVALIST 4
THE DOOMSAYER

'Tell the president what your team of seismologists has determined, Sissy,' Rourke directed to the woman standing to his left.

'Well, Mr. President, we've begun picking up readings on what appear to be a broad artificially created fault line – probably a result of the bombing on the Night of the War. Anytime now, there will be a massive quake, similar to the one along the San Andreas line that caused California to separate from the Continental plate. The Florida Peninsula will split from the Florida Panhandle and –'

'Mother of God!' the president broke in, sinking down in his chair.

'Evacuate as much of Florida as possible while there's still time,' Rourke advised.

'But,' the president began, wiping his forehead, 'the Cuban Communists control it. How can we intervene?'

'I think I know a way we can get it from the Russians,' said Rourke. 'And if we don't get some sort of truce for the duration of this thing – this may be the greatest loss of lives in recorded history, with the exception of the Night of the War.'

The president, his eyes glassy and hard-set, stared up at Rourke. 'Go on, Rourke,' he said. 'Let's hear your idea.'

*The Survivalist series by Jerry Ahern,
published by New English Library*

THE SURVIVALIST 4
THE DOOMSAYER

Jerry Ahern

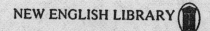
NEW ENGLISH LIBRARY

First published in the USA in 1981 by Kensington Publishing Corporation

First NEL Paperback Edition February 1984
Reprinted March 1984
Reprinted September 1984
Reprinted March 1985
Reprinted March 1986

NEL Books are published by
New English Library,
Mill Road, Dunton Green,
Sevenoaks, Kent.
Editorial office: 47 Bedford Square, London WC1B 3DP

Made and printed in Great Britain by
Hunt Barnard Printing Ltd., Aylesbury, Bucks.

British Library C.I.P.

Ahern, Jerry
  The doomsayer.—(The Survivalist; 4)
  I. Title   II. Series
  813'.54[F]   PS3551.H/

  ISBN 0-450-05660-0

Chapter 1

Rourke closed the Lowe Alpine Loco Pack and checked that it was secure on the back of the jet-black Harley Davidson Low Rider. He scanned the ground in the early sunlight and checked that the fire was out and all his gear accounted for. He would need gasoline by the end of the day and was aiming toward one of the strategic fuel reserve sites the new President of United States II, Samuel Chambers, had pinpointed for him. He had been out of the Retreat for nearly seven days, having re-equipped, then waited a day more while Paul Rubenstein had prepared. He left the same day Paul had set out for Florida in quest of his parents to see if somehow they had survived the holocaust of the Night of the War—World War III. "World War Last?" he wondered, noting the haze around the sunrise, the redness of the atmosphere. The Geiger counter strapped to the Harley still indicated normal radiation levels, but John Thomas Rourke was worried.

In the seven days he had been out there had been no sign of Sarah, his wife, nor of his children, Michael and Ann.

He was heading east, assuming that Sarah and the children had for some reason turned toward the Georgia coast, perhaps to avoid Brigand bands or the Russians. On this gamble Rourke currently hung his slim hopes. He had missed them before by mere hours.

He snatched up the CAR-15, popped out the thirty-round magazine, worked the bolt, and removed the chambered round there. Then he loaded the .223 solid into the magazine and snapped off the trigger, putting the magazine back up the well. He bent his head as he slung the collapsible-stock semiautomatic rifle across his back, muzzle down, scope covers in place.

He kicked away the stand on the Harley and started it, the humming of the engine somehow reassuring to him. He had chosen the Harley before the War because he had felt it was the best—and it hadn't let him down. Like the Rolex Submariner on his wrist, the Colt rifle on his back, the Detonics pistols in the double shoulder rig under his brown leather jacket, the six-inch Colt Python on his right hip—with these weapons he had survived until now.

He stared past the bike into the gorge below, and his eyes followed the road climbing the side of the gorge from near the river bottom.

Was Rubenstein alive? Had he yet located his parents? They were somewhere in the Armageddon that was Florida—like the rest of the United States, but only worse because there the Communist Cubans reportedly ruled at the discretion of the Soviets, titular winners of the War. Sarah, his son Michael, his daughter Ann. . . . Soon, Rourke thought, they would be turning—Michael was nearly seven, Ann almost five.

Rourke revved the machine under him and started forward out of the small clearing where he had camped the night, following the mountains as long as he could before dropping to the Piedmont. He looked for some sign of a camp, hoofprints from the horses Sarah and the children had ridden as they had left Tennessee in search of him. Rourke pushed the sunglasses up against the bridge of his nose as he turned the bike from the clearing onto the winding animal trail that lead out of the woods.

Rourke slowed the bike again at the edge of the tree line, cutting it in a narrow arc and stopping, surveying the gorge more clearly visible now below him, snapping up the leather jacket's collar against the cold—it was summer by the calendar. The oddity of the seasons worried him, too.

He could hear the rushing of water, but it was not that noise which caused him to cut the Harley's motor and listen, hardly daring to breathe. A smile crossed his lips. Rourke lit one of the small, dark tobacco cigars in the blue-yellow flame of his Zippo and listened more intently, inhaling the gray smoke then exhaling it hard through his nostrils.

Gunfire, engine noises. The Brigands, Rourke thought, below him along the road paralleling the gorge. He dismounted the bike, letting out the kick stand, and walked toward the lip of ground looking down into the river bottom canyon. He snatched the Bushnell Armored 8x30s from the case under his jacket and focused them along the road below.

A single motorcycle, the rider low over the handlebars; and a hundred yards or less behind the rider were two dozen or so motorcycles. Behind them, at a short distance, were a half-dozen pickup trucks—filled with Brigands. He focused in on the rider of the lead motorcycle. A woman with reddish-brown hair that hung straight in the slipstream behind her.

He watched. The woman rounded a curve, the bike skidding from under her, out of control.

She pulled herself to her feet, the Brigands closing in. They would want her for rape, for robbery, and then for murder, Rourke thought. The girl had the bike up and was getting it started again. The Brigand pursuers were less than thirty yards behind her now, and there was gunfire again. As she straightened the bike on the road below Rourke, he could see her twitch as a pistol shot echoed among the rocks, see her back arch, the bike weave, then see her lean over the handlebars, lower than before. He focused in more tightly on her— her left hand was streaming blood from some wound elsewhere on her body.

Rourke swept the binoculars back down the road. The Brigand gang closed in on her, their guns firing, some of them armed with submachineguns. Men and women stood in the pickup truck beds speeding behind the bikers, firing rifles at the girl cyclist.

Rourke carefully but quickly replaced the binoculars in their case, slipping the Colt CAR-15 from his back, the sling now on his right shoulder. He grasped the ears on the bolt and chambered the first round from the thirty-round magazine, then worked the safety to on.

Slowly, deliberately, he walked back to his own Harley, swung his right leg across and settled himself, then kicked away the stand. "Damn it," he rasped to himself. He gunned the Low Rider along the edge of the tree line, scanning the ground for a suitable access to the gorge below.

The path down into the gorge was steep and the gravel and dirt loose beneath the Harley's wheels as Rourke balanced himself, his feet dragging as he headed his machine down into the gorge. The sound of the gunfire was louder now, the face of the girl clearly visible as she looked up and then back at the pursuing Brigand killers.

Something in his fleeting glimpse of her face had told him she was pretty.

Rourke hit the level of the gorge road. The Harley bounced over a hummock of hard-packed clay and stone, and the bike came down hard, Rourke's jaw set against the impact. The wind of the slipstream as he accelerated the Harley blew the hair from his forehead. He raced the bike ahead to intercept the girl, putting distance between himself and the nearest of the Brigand bikers, now less than a dozen yards behind him along the river.

Rourke leaned low over his machine, throttling it out, the ripping and tearing sound of the exhaust from the engine reassuring in its strength, its very loudness. He was gaining on the girl. She was low over her bike and at an awkward angle. Gunshots echoed behind him from the Brigand bikers and the pickup trucks following them. Rourke swung the CAR-15 forward, thumbing off the safety, pointing the rifle behind him, firing it without looking back at his pursuers. A little gunfire might slow them, he thought—only a fool was eager to die.

He swung the rifle back at his side, thumbing the

safety on, throttling out his bike. The brown-haired girl was less than ten yards ahead of him now, the Japanese bike she rode seemingly at full throttle. There was a burst of gunfire—an automatic weapon, Rourke determined—and he swerved his bike far left toward the edge of the road and the river bank. The girl ahead of him lurched—he could see the impact of the weapons-fire in the road, against the seat of the bike she rode, against her body. She slumped low over the machine, the bike weaving.

The road twisted ahead of him, Rourke keeping his Harley at full throttle in spite of it, closing the gap between himself and the wounded girl. Five yards, four, six feet, five. Three feet—he was beside her now.

Rourke swung his rifle back out of the way on the sling, then reached out with his right arm. The girl's face turned up toward him, her lips drawn back, her teeth bared against the wind, her eyes filled with fear. Rourke hooked his right arm toward her, catching her under the right armpit, his hand squeezing around her, brushing against the fullness of her breast. He cut the bike he rode left, pulling the girl from her motorcycle, shouting to her across the wind, "Get on! Hurry!"

He could feel her moving as he fought to balance the Harley. He edged forward to give her added room, felt her suddenly behind him, her arms encircling his waist and her hands pressed against his chest. Rourke throttled out the Harley as the Japanese bike the girl had ridden zoomed toward him. It missed him and spun out over the edge of the road and past the river bank, rocketing into the water.

Both hands on the bars, Rourke cut back on his speed, making a wide right angle into the bend of the road and starting the Harley to climb. The gunfire behind him picked up in intensity. The sound of the girl's labored breathing in his left ear was somehow audible to him despite the roar of the Harley's engine. He could feel her head lolling against him and rasped, "Hold on, damn it!"

He scanned the road ahead of them—it climbed steeply and sharply out of the gorge, potholed and uneven and twisting. Rourke set his jaw and squinted against the sunlight as he gunned the bike ahead.

Chapter 2

Rourke gunned his Harley glancing over his shoulder as the Brigand gunfire crackled from behind him. Then he turned his eyes back to the sharp shoulder of the gorge straight ahead of him. The girl's breathing was hard in his ear now, the moaning of pain from her gunshot wounds unmistakable to him. His black-booted feet balancing the big bike, he hauled it up, over a hummock of ground and onto the narrow ridge. Rourke wrestled the Harley to his left and started along the shoulder of ground—the grating of truck and motorcycle gears, the belching of exhausts, the Brigand gunfire was all too near, he realized.

Rourke guided his bike along the ridge for a quarter mile, the pickups along the embankment, the Brigand motorcycles behind him. Spotting a particularly steep channel of red clay and gravel leading back down to the road, Rourke throttled back on the Harley and wheeled the machine left. He crossed less than a yard from the lead Brigand pickup truck, snatching one of the Detonics .45s into his left hand and snapping off two shots fast into the truck's windshield. As Rourke headed the bike down toward the road, ramming the cocked and locked Detonics into his belt under his jacket, he glanced to his left—the pickup truck was out of control, rolling over and careening down the embankment. Rourke gunned the Harley as the pickup truck exploded. The heat of the fireball scorched his face as he glanced back. Then he jumped the Harley onto the road.

Rourke heard the girl, her voice weak as she tried to shout: "Who are you?" Shaking his head, Rourke throttled out the bike, then glanced behind him. The Brigand bikers had already reached the road, and a second pickup crashed into the first. There was another explosion. Rourke leaned forward over his bike. The river road veered sharply upward ahead and Rourke took it, throttling down as he started into the grade. Then he increased his speed as he kept the Harley just to the right of the black top road's fading yellow line. Over seventy as he hauled the bike toward the top of the grade, Rourke let the machine out as the road leveled. Glancing behind him, he saw nearly a dozen Brigand bikers. They were coming up over the rise in pursuit, behind them a half-dozen trucks.

Rourke looked ahead, then behind again as automatic weapons fire chipped into the pavement all around him. There were men and women standing in the pickup trucks, firing assault rifles over the cab roofs. Rourke retrieved the Detonics from his belt, wiping down the safety with his right thumb, turning awkwardly in the bike saddle with the woman behind him. His right arm stretched to maximum extension; he fired the stainless .45 once, then again. One of the lead bikers swerved. Rourke fired twice more, emptying the shiny pistol. The biker spun out, up the lip of concrete on the right side of the road, the man's body soaring high into the trees. There was a scream, resonating over the crackle of gunfire as Rourke rammed the slide-opened pistol awkwardly into his belt and bent low again over his bike, taking it into a sharp, almost hairpinning curve.

The road dropped off now to the right, and at the bottom of a long-running, nearly overgrown grade was a stream. Rourke cut the bike into a hard right, dropping his speed, his feet skidding along the road surface as he pulled the bike up and over the runoff gutter, then onto the dirt of the grade. The Harley skidded under him, his right leg going out, bracing the machine as his arms strained to right the black bike between his legs. His lips drawn back, his teeth bared, Rourke shouted to the wounded girl still holding on behind him, "Hang on!"

The gunfire from behind him abruptly stopped for a moment as Rourke angled the bike diagonally across the grade. Then he looked up. Two of the pickup trucks were already starting down, trailing six of the bikers. The remaining pickups were parked along the edge of the road, and in an instant there was gunfire again from the Brigands.

Rourke turned the bike hard right to miss a deadfall tree trunk. The machine started to skid away from him, but his fists knotted on the handlebars, pulling the machine upright as he braced against its weight with his left leg, his boots dragging the ground. The bike under control again, Rourke throttled out, jumping over another deadfall and away from the grade and onto the bank of the fast-running but shallow stream. Some of the Brigand bikers had already made it down, Rourke saw now, glancing behind him. Then he throttled out and headed toward the stream. It was shallow, rocky—perfect he thought, as he cut the handlebars to his right and the bike half-jumped, half-wheeled into the water. His feet bracing the machine, he upped his speed. Icy water splashed up past his calves, spraying against his face as the front tire of the Harley sliced through the stream.

More gunfire sent bullets ricocheting off the water around him. Rourke glanced back. There were still five bikers and two trucks. Wrenching the front of the bike up hard, the machine almost wholly supported on his legs as he reached the far bank, Rourke gunned up and out of the water. Flipping off the CAR-15's safety, he swung the rifle up, his right fist wrapped on the pistol grip. He fired a two-round burst, then another and another. The lead biker's machine slammed hard against a large rock in the center of the stream, the biker soaring upward, hands clasped to his face. Rourke turned away, starting the Harley up the incline of red clay and gravel, back toward the river road.

As the Harley reached the top of the grade, Rourke could already hear—almost feel—that the remaining Brigands had doubled back. As he hit the road edge, Rourke made the bike surge ahead. The CAR-15 back in his right fist, he fired as the Brigand pickups that had stayed on the road bore down on him. Crossing in front of them, he emptied his rifle. One of the pickup trucks and two of the bikers collided as Rourke took the far grade the only way he could. He could feel it more than see it, the bike in mid-air, the wheels spinning and the engine noise almost deafening as he throttled back. Then the bike impacted. His spine, his neck, his shoulders—the bones themselves shuddered as he wrestled the big machine to keep it from skidding under him.

"Lost it," he snarled, feeling the girl's hands letting loose of him, feeling the Harley slide from between his legs. Rolling, snatching at the second of the twin stainless Detonics .45s, Rourke came up on his knees. His hands were sore and bloodied as he shoved the .45 straight ahead of him, thumb cocking the hammer, his right trigger finger edging back. The pistol bucked once, then once more in his hands—the lead biker coming down the grade and catching both rounds. The man's hands sprung out from the handlebars, his face twisted in pain and surprise, the bike going on, down the grade. The body of the already dead biker hit the grade spread-eagled, sliding downward. Then a second biker crashed into the first man's body, his bike rocking out of control, sending the rider sprawling face forward into the dirt.

Rourke was on his feet, his left hand grasping the woman's shoulders, dragging her toward the Harley as he fired out the .45 with his right hand.

"Hang on—come on!" Rourke snapped, righting the bike. He silently prayed he hadn't damaged it as he gunned the engine, balancing the machine between his legs and starting off toward the river bank.

Rourke glanced behind him. One of the pickup trucks hit the road edge too fast, sailing off into mid-air. As he turned away he could hear the explosion at impact sound. The girl behind him screamed. Ahead, perhaps five hundred yards along the river bank, Rourke saw their chance. There were still three bikers behind him as he shot a glance back. Two pickups, guns blazing from the truck beds, were slowly taking the grade down from the road.

Rourke throttled out the bike, already gauging the distance from the river bank to the auto ferry moored there. Perhaps a dozen feet. He tried judging the length of the ferry, the length of the run along the river bank. With two hundred yards to go, Rourke swung the CAR-15 out of his way then rasped to the girl, "Whatever happens, hold on, then let go when I shout—just do it!" At one hundred yards Rourke swung the Harley left to the farthest extreme of the river bank. He judged the distance between the bank and the auto ferry as greater now—perhaps eighteen feet. One heavy rope was tied to a stout pine some five or six feet back from the near edge of the river bank. Fifty yards. Rourke worked out a scenario in his mind to explain the presence of the auto ferry. Brigands perhaps, perhaps someone else. Whoever had last used the ferry had taken it downriver and, possibly with an eye to future use, secured it along the river bank.

Twenty-five yards now and Rourke dropped his speed as he widened his arc and edged away from the water. Eighteen feet, he decided—the jump would be eighteen feet from the river bank to the auto ferry, more dangerous because it was so short and the power and acceleration he'd need to make it might carry him too far. The ferry's length was about thirty feet from end to end. Ten feet remaining before the jump and Rourke shouted to the girl behind him, "Hold on—tight!"

His jaw set, Rourke wheeled the bike, aiming it straight for the river bank, the Harley bumping and jostling over the rough ground. Rourke's hands gripped the handlebars like a pair of vices, his eyes already focused on the auto ferry deck. He revved the Harley Davidson, pulling up on the front end by the handlebars, and the bike jumped out over the water, the rear end dropping. The front end was too high, Rourke thought. Then the rear wheel crashed onto the deck. Throwing his weight forward to get steering control from the front wheel, Rourke roared to the girl, "Jump clear—jump—now!"

Rourke braked the Harley hard, the bike skidding. And above the screeching sound and the exhaust noises there was still the gunfire. The bike slipped, still sliding and Rourke with it toward the far end of the deck. The wooden planks were rough against Rourke's hands and legs, tearing at him. He twisted the machine, hauling at it, trying to slow it. The bike finally stopped and Rourke with it. He looked up, his hands bleeding, his arms aching. The Harley was less than six inches from the edge of the auto ferry's deck.

Rourke clambered to his feet, snatching at the CAR-15, dumping the empty thirty-round magazine, ramming a fresh one home. He worked the bolt and ran back across the ferry, the gun already spitting fire in his hands.

Rourke reached the rope securing the ferry to the river bank, shouting to the injured girl, "Secure my bike if you can!" The A.G. Russell black chrome Sting IA was in his left hand, the double-edged blade hacking at the rope.

Already, the remaining Brigand cyclists were roaring up along the river bank. Rourke hacked again with the knife blade, the rope fraying and snapping as the current tugged at the auto ferry. The flat-decked river boat pulled away from the bank now and into the current. Rourke telescoped out the stock on the CAR-15, ripping the scope covers away. He sighted on the nearest Brigand biker, firing the CAR-15 almost as soon as the cross hairs settled. "One," he snarled, the first biker going down.

Rourke swung the muzzle along the river bank. "Two," he whispered as he fired again, the second biker sprawling back off his machine, the motorcycle spinning itself out into the water. Rourke swung the muzzle of the CAR-15. There were two pickup trucks driving along the river bank. Rourke sighted on the driver of the first truck. "Tough shot," he muttered, then drew his trigger finger back, the rifle cracking but not really moving. Another reason he liked the .223, he thought, was that he could ride out recoil when he wanted to, since with the straight-line stock of the CAR-15 recoil was almost non-existent.

Rourke followed the pickup truck cab through the three-power scope as the driver pawed at the wheel with one arm. Rourke fired again. Through the scope he was able to see the bright red flower of blood on the side of the neck, matching the one already on the driver's right arm. The driver's head snapped back, and the truck cut left, slamming into the river bank, then bouncing toward the water. Already, the Brigand men and women in the truck bed were jumping clear. "No," Rourke rasped under his breath, swinging the scope onto the escaping Brigands. He fired once, twice, three times, then a two-round burst, catching some of them in mid-air as they flipped from the back of the truck. He hit some of them as they ran off after jumping to the ground.

Rourke raised the muzzle of the rifle, the rest of the surviving Brigands fleeing from the river bank. The rifle had done for Rourke what he'd wanted it to do—he had no desire for a running gun battle between the ferry and the river bank.

He turned and stared at the girl with the reddish-brown hair. She was pale, he thought. Then he started toward her in long, loping strides, breaking into a run, the CAR-15 swinging to his side as he tried to catch her before she collapsed over the side of the ferry and into the current. Rourke got both hands under her armpits and pulled her against him. But she was already unconscious and—he confirmed it now—the left arm was still streaming blood. He moved his right hand across her back, finding a bullet wound there as well. The sticky feeling of blood was something he couldn't mistake.

Chapter 3

"I was the only one who knew how to ride a motorcycle, so I guess I was elected. I'd always talked about equality of the sexes—so here was my big chance. When your parents give you a first name like 'Sissy' you can't just sit around and be one."

Rourke looked at the girl, his eyes smiling. "So 'Sissy' had to prove she wasn't a sissy. And you could've gotten yourself killed. Or worse—and I mean that literally."

The girl winced a little as Rourke checked the security of the bandage on her left shoulder where a bullet had grazed her. "Lucky for me," she began, sucking in her breath hard as Rourke took the blanket back from her and probed at the wound along the left side of her rib cage. "Lucky you're a doctor."

"Lucky that bullet didn't break a couple of your ribs. It hit you at just the right angle and skated along between the second and third rib and lodged there. In a few days you'll feel fine. Time for that old joke about the guy who's injured, both hands damaged. Says to the doctor, 'You mean after the bandages come off, I'll be able to play the violin?' The doctor nods and the guy says, 'Wow—I could never play the violin before!' But you'll be fine—whatever you do," Rourke added.

"After I passed out, did I—ahh—" the girl stammered.

"What? That ahh of yours covers a wide range of possibilities. But no—all you did was stay passed out. I took the auto ferry downstream—I make it about twenty-five miles or so—and that's where I removed the bullet along your ribs. Then I decided it was safe to stop awhile. So here we are." Rourke gestured with his hands to the riverside clearing, a semicircle of bright green pines and a few naturally growing cedars at the far side. Beyond the trees were foothills.

"I didn't say anything then?" the girl asked again.

Rourke dropped to one knee beside her, studying her face. There was relief there, and pain too—but something else, uncertainty and fear.

"What shouldn't you have said?" Rourke asked, his voice low, the words slow.

"No—it's just—"

"I'm not going to suppose those Brigands were chasing you for any other reason besides the fact that you were alone and unarmed—and they like women that way especially. But why were you the only one who could ride a bike—what did you get elected to do?" Rourke asked.

"Just—some friends of mine. We were—up in the mountains ever since the War and we had to get— ahh—" and the girl stopped.

"Next time you say ahh, let me know in advance and I can get a tongue depresser out of the first-aid kit and check your tonsils," Rourke told her.

"I'm sorry," she smiled. "It's just that—ahh—" And she laughed, tears coming into the corners of her eyes a second later as she reached for her left rib cage.

"I forgot to mention you shouldn't laugh," Rourke said slowly.

"I just promised—"

"Here." Rourke fished into his hip pocket and took out his wallet, opened the plastic bag sealing it, and searched inside. In a moment he passed her a plastic coated identity card with his photo on it.

"C.I.A.?"

"Retired. I don't even think there is a C.I.A. any more. I guess what I'm trying to get across is you can trust me—if you need to."

Rourke took one of his small, dark tobacco cigars and lit it in the blue-yellow flame of his Zippo. "Well?" he asked her.

"I'm Sissy Wiznewski—*Doctor* Wiznewski, really. I'm a kind of geologist," she began.

"What kind of geologist?"

"Seismology. We—Dr. Jarvis, Dr. Tanagura, Peter Krebbs, and I—we were manning a survey station up in the mountains."

"I don't follow you," Rourke said matter-of-factly.

"Well, I don't know if you know it," she began again, "but there are—"

"Fault lines around here," Rourke interrupted. "But the strength of any shocks in the area has been minor so far."

"Right—that's true. That's why we were here. We

25

were recording plate tectonics to compare with plate movement in California and along the West Coast. You may have read or seen something on television about how scientists are trying to figure ways of defusing earthquakes before stress between plates gets so severe that one plate slips and there's a major earthquake."

"So," Rourke said thoughtfully, studying the girl's face—she had green eyes. "So you were studying plate movement here to get a handle on what—other than geologic age—has contributed to stability and to learn what you could engineer into this defusing process."

"Yeah," she interrupted him. "Exactly. So we could learn what we might be able to do to stabilize plate movement on the West Coast. If we investigated the end result of a quiescent fault system then we might learn what sort of things we could do to relieve plate tensions on the West Coast."

"Was it working?" Rourke asked her.

"Yes—I think so. I mean, all the preliminary data we were accumulating seemed to indicate our research was going along the right direction and everything. But it was really too early to tell, then there was the—" The girl stopped, turning her face away to stare at the ground.

"What? Were you sort of like Noah's dove—they sent you out to see if there were still a world left?"

"No," she answered, her voice so soft Rourke could barely hear it. He guessed the girl was about twenty-seven or twenty-eight. And Rourke also guessed there was something that was frightening her, more terribly than the pursuit of the Brigands or even the War itself.

"You discovered something, something that couldn't

wait any longer," he surmised.

"Yes—we did. It was really an accident, but we're certain about the findings, at least as certain as we can be without field investigation on the spot. I don't know if that's possible. We figured somebody had to tell the Army, or even if the Russians had won the War, tell them. Somebody had to do something. And there isn't time to wait."

"Tell them what?" Rourke asked her, studying the glowing reddish tip of his cigar.

"Who won the War?" The girl looked at him, her eyes wide.

"We all lost—the Soviets have some troops over here, but . . . You're a scientist, you should see that better than I do. If it's summer now—then why are we wearing heavy clothes, why has the temperature been dipping to the freezing mark at night? What did you find?"

"Tell me one thing first—was the West Coast bombed heavily."

"You have people there?"

"Yes, but—from a scientific standpoint, I need to know. Do you know?"

"Apparently the fault line ruptured under the impact of the explosions there—the old fears about California slipping off into the sea. Well," Rourke sighed, "it happened—there is no West Coast anymore. None— it's gone."

The girl made the sign of the cross, staring down at the ground, heavy sobbing her only response to his words.

Rourke stood up, walking toward the river bank, studying the water, the tip of his cigar, the toes of his black combat boots. He heard her voice behind him, the words difficult to understand through the sounds of her tears. "Did they bomb Florida?" But the girl didn't wait for him to answer as he turned to face her. He watched as she stared straight ahead into the trees. "Well—then we're right. The night of the bombing."

"The Night of the War?" Rourke almost whispered.

"The bombing did something that shouldn't have been possible, but it created an artificial fault line—I guess you'd call it that. The instruments we had implanted all up and down the coast went insane when the bombs dropped that night. But they were built to withstand massive shock and most of them held up. We then found a fault line that wasn't there before the War, gradually growing. It could be days from now, just a few, but it could also be hours. There's going to be an earthquake, one of the most massive ever recorded. There could be thousands of people killed. Maybe millions. I don't know how many people there are down there since the War began. But soon—" The girl sobbed heavily. Rourke took a few steps nearer to her, then dropped to one knee beside her. "Soon, there's going to be an earthquake along that new fault line, and it will separate the Florida peninsula from the rest of the continent and the peninsula will crash down into the sea. There should be tidal waves all along the coast, into the Gulf too. But the whole Florida Peninsula will disappear from the face of the earth."

The girl looked up at him, turning around awkwardly because of her wounds. Rourke saw something pleading in her eyes and he folded her into his arms, letting her cry against his chest. "So many, so many people—Jesus," the girl cried.

Rourke looked down into the girl's hair, then over his shoulder toward the ferry boat. The motorcycle on the deck was almost completely out of gasoline after the high-speed chase. "Paul," Rourke whispered. "My God . . ."

Rourke let the girl cry for a while—the tension of everything that had happened to her demanded it, he realized. He guessed she'd been close to some of the people who had died in the San Andreas quake that had wiped out California. And now she saw it happening all over again. She said nothing else yet, but Rourke realized now why she had been sent by the others of her team. The knowledge of the impending disaster had forced them to do something. Rourke wondered silently if Cuba or perhaps the Russians could be somehow alerted to help in the evacuation. Certainly the government of United States II should be told. All three had a stake in the population of Florida. Rourke wondered how many men, women, and children had survived the Night of the War, the reported Communist Cuban occupation.

There was his own search for Sarah and the children to consider. But perhaps they would be near the coast where the tidal waves provide a built-in warning as the tides begin rising. There would at least be a chance for them, Rourke thought. But his friend Paul Ruben-stein was likely in Florida by now. There would be no chance for him. Rourke thought about the young man. Before the Night of the War, neither had known the other existed. And in the space of a few hours after the crash of the diverted jetliner they had all ridden, Rourke and Paul Rubenstein—ultimately the only two survivors from the passengers and crew—had begun

29

the friendship that had carried them across two-thirds of the United States. Rourke suddenly realized he had no idea why the New York City-based editor with a trade magazine had been in Canada to begin with and headed toward Atlanta. Rourke shook his head, a smile crossing his lips.

Rourke thought about himself a moment. He had made few friends in his life, had always had few relatives. "Friends," he whispered under his breath. Sarah, his wife, had always been his friend—perhaps that was why they had argued so much before the War, wasting hours they hadn't bothered to tally. Natalia— his most curious friend, he thought. He remembered their meeting in Texas that had led to Rourke's having a final showdown with her KGB husband, killing him. Rourke realized she probably hated him now. The one friend was Paul Rubenstein.

"I'll help you," Rourke whispered to the girl, her head against his chest and her sobbing subsiding now. "We can take the ferry boat downriver. I think I can find a contact in Army Intelligence in Savannah. We can do something to try to get some of the people out before it happens. I don't really know how much we can do, how many people can be evacuated—however it's done. But you and your colleagues were right," he told her. "Something has to be done. And I guess now it's up to both of us."

The girl looked up at him, her green eyes still wet with tears, her face paler than it should have been. Rourke decided it was the loss of blood, the shock of the bullet wounds she'd sustained. He wondered how his own face looked. But it was a decision he had to make, he realized. The immediate search for Sarah,

Michael, and Ann—his family. Perhaps Paul was like a brother he'd never had, Rourke thought, smiling, amused at himself. He remembered Sarah once telling him that it was cold-blooded to plan for survival if most of your fellow men could not survive. Their perennial argument over his preparation for disaster and her optimism concerning world peace had been forever resolved on the Night of the War when bitter reality had proven his case. But the one thing he'd never been able to make her understand was that he had no illusions that survival alone would be survival. It was the enlightened self-interest of love that made him search for Sarah and his two children, Rourke realized. And it was the "selfishness" of friendship that compelled him now to find Paul Rubenstein. Rourke had buried his father years earlier, his mother not long after that. If the Night of the War had taught him anything, Rourke thought, it was that a human life was too precious not to fight for.

Chapter 4

Sarah Rourke rested her hands on the saddle horn. Tildie's head dipped down as the horse browsed at a patch of grass. Sarah's eyes scanned the valley beneath the low hill on which they'd stopped. She looked behind her. Michael sat easily in the saddle of her husband's big off-white horse, Sam. She smiled at little Annie, the girl waving to her. Shaking her head, almost not believing the children could have endured what they had, she studied her hands. The nails were trimmed short and there was dirt under them. She had always kept her nails long, even with the farm, the children, the horses, her illustrating. At least the nails on her left hand had been nearly perfect, she thought, smiling. She looked at the gold wedding band, wondering if somewhere still in the world its mate was on a living hand like her own. She cooed to the horse under her as it started to move, raising both her hands to the nape of her neck to retie the blue and white bandanna over her hair. Was John Rourke actually alive? she wondered.

Mary Mulliner's farm, she remembered. She could have stayed there, forever if she had wanted to, the children having an island of normality in the world or what was left of it. But she had packed the saddlebags, the dufflebag, cleaned the assault rifle she'd taken from one of the men who'd tried to rape and kill her. She'd gotten Mary's red-headed son to show her how to "field strip"—that was what he had called it—the rifle and her husband's Colt .45 automatic. She'd saddled her own horse that morning. Annie had cried, and Michael had talked of how he would take care of Annie, and his mother as well. It was summer now, though by the weather she realized she would have never guessed that. Turning and looking at her two children, she murmured, "Michael will be seven." She shook her head in disbelief. Six years old and he had killed a man to save her life; six years old and the boy had saved her life again after she'd drunk contaminated water. The corners of her gray-green eyes crinkled with a smile— the resemblance between Michael and his father wasn't just physical. She studied the boy's face, the dark eyes, the thick, dark hair. The forehead was lower; but Michael was still a boy, she reminded herself. The shoulders, the leanness about him. But it was the strength the boy seemed to have inside of him that at once heartened and sometimes terrified her. He was John all over—loving, analytical, practical, yet a dreamer too. It had taken the War, she realized, to understand that John Rourke's preoccupation with survivalism had not been nightmarish, but a dream for going on when civilization itself failed. She smiled again. She could no more see the War or its aftermath killing her husband John than it had killed Michael— and Michael was here, with her now.

"Michael," she said, looking at the boy with a smile on her lips.

He smiled back at her, saying, "Why are you smiling like that?"

"I love you." She looked over at Annie. "And I love you, too."

"We know that," the boy said, starting to laugh.

"I know you know," she laughed. Then she pulled up on Tildie's reins and said over her shoulder to the children, "Come on kids—"

She stopped, reining in, the internal terror gripping at her again, thinking, "Come on—where?" Shaking her head, she let out on the reins, moving her knees against Tildie's warm flanks again. "Come on," she said aloud, starting the mare down into the valley.

They rode in relative quiet for more than an hour as she judged it by the sun still far to the east. After she had left the Mulliner farm she had tried heading into Georgia. But there had been Brigands, too many of them, she'd thought, to wait it out or skirt around them. She had made the decision then to turn East into the Carolinas, trying to reenter Georgia as she judged she had almost two days ago, nearer the Atlantic Coast. She had convinced herself that perhaps Savannah still existed as an entity, too important as a seaport to bomb from existence. She reined in on Tildie again, staring now across the low valley, then back behind her into the hills. Before the War, she thought, the sound of an automobile or truck engine had been familiar, sometimes comforting. She had liked it when someone had stopped by the farm unexpectedly—at least most of the time. There would be the rumbling, humming noise, and she would look out the window of her studio or through the kitchen windows and see a familiar vehicle pulling up the driveway. Since the War the sound of engines had meant only one thing to her— Brigands.

"Children!" she almost shrieked. "Hurry up!" She kicked her heels into Tildie's sides, bending around in the saddle, watching Michael as he dropped low over his horse's neck, and Annie as she slapped her tiny hands against her horse's rump. The two children moved their mounts ahead. "Hurry," she called again, her right hand moving from Tildie's mane to the butt of her husband's Government Model .45 jammed in the waistband of her faded Levis. In the valley where they rode, they were in the open, exposed.

She could pinpoint the source of the sound now, just over the hills leading down into the valley. The only shelter up ahead was a farmhouse. "Over there!" she finally shouted, wishing the children could make their animals move more quickly, wishing she hadn't let Annie try riding by herself. The girl wasn't yet five, wouldn't be for four more months. "Come on, children," she said again, staring back toward the hills, the engine sounds getting louder, more well defined. Trucks, many of them—and there was another sort of sound. She had ridden with John on his motorcycle, she had heard motorcycles ever since the War, and she heard them now.

"Brigands," she almost screamed to the children. "Hurry! For God's sake—" And under her breath as she drew in on the reins, Tildie backing up a step, the children almost even with her now, Sarah whispered, "For our sake!"

She stared toward the hills, the engine noises getting louder, then turned her head quickly, watching the children's mounts heading toward the farmhouse. She drew in tight on Tildie's reins, loosing the modified AR-15 from the saddle thongs, slinging it across her back. "Come on, girl," she snapped, heeling into the horse, bending low over its flowing mane as the dark hairs whipped her face in the wind, tears coming to her eyes because of it.

Sarah passed Annie's horse, swinging her right hand out and swatting the horse on the rump. Then she snatched at the reins, leading out the left rein as she pulled ahead on Tildie. Glancing behind her, first at Annie, then to the hills, Sarah thought she saw the profile of a truck or car coming into view. She shouted to Tildie, "Giddup! Come on, girl!" Michael was already starting to rein in, the farmhouse just ahead. "Michael!" Sarah shouted. "Get your horse inside— hurry!" Sarah, as Michael began dismounting, reined in old Tildie, swinging easily from the saddle, shifting the AR-15 on her back, snatching out with both hands for the reins of Annie's horse. She hauled the animal down, then grabbed the little girl from the saddle. "Run—into the house." Sarah pushed Michael ahead of her, holding the reins now of all three horses.

Michael was struggling with the farmhouse door. Sarah almost pushed the boy aside, throwing her weight against the door as she tried turning the knob, the rough unpainted wood scratching against her hands. But the door gave and she hurried Michael through, Annie after him. She could see over to the brow of the hill now—they weren't trucks. They were tanks, with red stars on their sides. "Russians," she rasped, swatting the horses in through the door ahead of her. She stepped through the door, swinging it shut, collapsing against it.

Sarah Rourke heard Michael call out, "Momma!"

She spun on her heels, the .45 automatic in her hand, her thumb pushing down the safety. Two ideas came to her as one—how conditioned she had become to danger, to defending herself and the children from it; and who was the man with the bloodstained shirt, a revolver falling from his limp right hand as he collapsed onto the floor from a cot in the corner. He had what she'd learned was a South Georgia accent as he rasped, "I'm with the Resistance. . . ."

As Sarah started toward him across the floor, she realized there were Russians outside her door—but there was a new, unwanted responsibility within.

Chapter 5

John Rourke watched as the needle of the Harley's fuel gauge hovered near the "E"—he made it another ten miles before he reached the site of the strategic fuel reserve, one of the sites pinpointed on the map given him by Samuel Chambers, the President of United States II. Rourke had memorized the map, then destroyed it, later reproducing a copy and storing it at the Retreat where Paul Rubenstein memorized it as well. This was the first time Rourke had found it necessary to tap into the fuel reserve supply—finding gasoline, stealing it, trading for it as he had gone along. But this was the farthest he had been from the Retreat as well.

He had taken the auto ferry as far as he dared toward Savannah, abandoning it and leaving the girl in as secure a spot as he could find. He did not want the injured girl to slow him as he made his way to the gasoline supply, nor would he unnecessarily endanger her. As best he knew, Soviet troops honeycombed the Savannah area, using it as a primary southeastern port facility now. And there were Brigands, as the earlier encounter attested. Rourke had left the woman the little Colt Lawman two incher as last ditch protection, as well as food and water in case something went wrong. There was a rise ahead and Rourke took the bike up, then over it. Checking the black-faced Rolex Submariner on his wrist, he made it another ten minutes before he reached the site given the current terrain—and remembering the map he didn't foresee the terrain improving. It was uneven, untraveled. All in all, Rourke reflected, a smile crossing his lips, the perfect location for a strategic oil and gas reserve. Off the beaten path, accessible by motorcycle or the heaviest of trucks. Rourke pitied the fuel tanker drivers who had traveled the rough road to bring the gasoline there originally.

After several more minutes driving the Harley, the needle fuel gauge settled well below Empty, and Rourke stopped the bike, the engine running a little rough, he thought. In his mind's eye he pinpointed the spot from the map, then checked his lensatic compass to make certain the coordinates he'd memorized were correct. He started the Harley Davidson down off the rise, slowly, the CAR-15 slung under his right arm. Rourke realized he was now at his most vulnerable. He could be stopped, in the open, the motorcycle unusable while he refueled then filled his emergency container. Rourke circled the big black bike around the clearing, then slowed it, cutting the wheel slightly left. He stopped, putting down the kick stand. Then he dismounted the bike, snapped back the bolt on the CAR-

15 and let it fly forward, chambering a round. Rourke thumbed on the safety and walked out to the clearing, checking the compass again against the memorized map. He spotted a likely stand of trees and walked toward it, pushing his way through the pine boughs several feet, then finding the valve.

Chambers had explained that the strategic fuel reserves shown on the map were emergency supplies as opposed to massive reserves for civilian, industrial, and military use. Because of their emergency nature, they had been designed to operate on air pressure rather than electricity. And that meant that the time to refuel an average full-sized automobile, for example, as Chambers had explained it, would be roughly ten to twelve minutes—a slow process. Rourke smiled at the thought. He wondered if he'd ever drive an "average automobile" again. He went back to the Harley, then walked the bike back toward the edge of the tree line and began the refueling process. Even with the vastly smaller tanks, including the auxiliary tank, the process still seemed interminable as Rourke worked the pump, leaving the key on to watch the fuel gauge. He realized that with air in the system and the nearly bone-dry tank he could easily make a mistake, assuming his tanks were full when in reality they weren't. As he fueled the Harley, then began working on his emergency container, he scanned the clearing and the crude road leading down and through it. He was still vulnerable.

Rourke froze, hearing something that chilled his spine—it was another human voice, the words unmistakably Russian. It was cool, clear and there was a strong wind blowing from the direction from which he'd come, and despite the apprehension gripping

Rourke now, he continued the fueling operation. The voice came from beyond the low ridge over which he'd entered the clearing. Rourke calculated the situation—there were at least two men, probably an advance Soviet patrol. Rourke swung the CAR-15 forward, telescoping out the stock. He glanced at the emergency fuel container—it was almost full. He tightened the gas cap on the Harley Davidson, visually inspecting the area to make certain he'd left no other signs of his presence beyond the tire tracks. He'd spilled a few drops of fuel and he kicked dirt over the damp spots in the ground. The container was full and Rourke stopped pumping. Quickly, his eyes riveted through his dark aviator-style sunglasses to the ridge, Rourke sealed the emergency container, securing it on the Harley.

He coiled the pump hose back into its base, then shut down the valve, working the combination lock to secure it—Chambers had given Rourke the combination, too, at the time Rourke had received the map.

He heard the Russian voice more clearly now, closer. Moving the bike without starting it toward the center of the clearing, he went back over the ground and obliterated any footprints or tread marks as best he could, using the leather jacket he'd stripped from his back. Shouldering back into the jacket, reslinging the CAR-15 and collapsing the stock, Rourke mounted the motorcycle and waited. If the voice came no closer, he would wait until it was no longer audible, then go up to the ridge and, when all seemed clear, steal away. It was of paramount importance not to attract too much attention to the clearing and cause the Soviets to initiate a detailed search for the fuel reserve.

He could hear the voice clearly now, saying something in Russian about having followed tire tracks. A smile crossed Rourke's lips. Quickly, he dug into the Lowe pack on the back of the Harley, dismounting the bike then and gathering together some twigs and branches. Using the Zippo after skinning shavings off several of the twigs with his knife, Rourke started the twigs burning, setting out a pack of Mountain House food from the back pack on the ground. He crouched beside the small fire, waiting. If the Russians came over the ridge, they would see the campfire—and Rourke would hopefully convince them he had stopped for a meal. If he gave them a reason why he was there to begin with, then there might be no reason for the Russians to search further. He stared at the ridgeline, ripping open the Mountain House food pack. It was Turkey Tetrazini, and he scooped a handful of the dehydrated food into his hand, nibbling at it, letting the moisture of his mouth react with it to get the taste.

"No sense wasting all of it," he muttered to himself.

Finally Rourke heard a second voice—he'd begun to think the Russian on the other side of the ridge was neurotic, talking to himself. He could hear the conversation reasonably well now—the two voices were saying the tracks led up over the ridge.

Shaking his head, Rourke slung the CAR-15 across his back, muzzle down, safety on. He took the Metalifed six-inch Colt Python from the flap holster on his belt and pulled back on the cylinder release catch, spinning the cylinder once, checking that the ejector rod was tight. He closed the cylinder, his right fist wrapped around the black rubber Colt Medallion Pachmayr Grips, the long vent-ribbed barrel resting across his left thigh. And he munched at more of the Turkey Tetrazini, waiting for what he knew now was inevitable.

He squinted against the sunlight, feeling the heat of the small fire near his hands, hoping the Russians would hurry. A smile crossed his lips. Over the ridge-line he could see the crown of a Soviet foraging cap, then the head under it.

He stared at the face; the Russian stared back. There was a cry of alarm, and the Russian started to swing his AK-47 into position. Rourke, still squatting beside the fire, swung the Python up on line, the butt of the pistol in both his hands, the silvery front sight lining up dead center in the white outline Omega square notch. He pulled the trigger through, double action, the muzzle rising slightly as the revolver discharged. "Love that Mag-Na-Porting," he muttered to himself, the recoil from the full house .357 158-grain semi-jacketed soft point almost negligible. Rourke was on his feet then, running.

As he reached the Harley Davidson, jumping into the saddle, knocking away the stand, he saw a second Russian coming over the ridgeline, an AK-47 in the man's hands. As the Russian started to fire, Rourke wingshot the Python, once, then again. The Soviet soldier fell back. Rourke replaced the Python in the holster, gunning the motorcycle. Gunfire started up behind him, chewing into the dirt around him as he bent low over the machine. The engine was running well again, he decided, as he hit the opposite ridgeline and jumped the bike over it, coming down in the dirt, gunning the machine and starting down toward a road perhaps two hundred yards ahead. He could hear vehicles behind him, shouts, gunfire—he still had no idea of the size of the Soviet patrol, but hoped they'd bought the campfire routine. As Rourke reached the road, he looked back along the river. There was a Soviet truck, small, camouflage-painted, coming toward him. He skidded the bike into a tight turn, stopping it, drawing the Python, thumbing back the hammer. The Russian vehicle was over the ridge. Rourke fired the Python, once, then twice more in rapid succession. There was a cloud of steam from the front of the truck, the vehicle stopped dead halfway over the ridge. Rourke dropped the Python back into the holster and gunned the Harley down the road. It was tree-lined, the branches almost touching over the road as he passed under them. He reached his left hand into his shirt pocket and found one of his small cigars. Biting down on it in the left corner of his mouth as he sped along the road, Rourke decided to light it later.

Chapter 6

General Varakov stood looking out from the mezzanine onto the main hall. Over the time he had used the lakeside Museum as his headquarters, since his arrival from Moscow shortly after the Night of the War, he had studied the skeletons of the mastadons, fighting and dominating the main hall of the Museum. Varakov smiled—it was either here or down by the lakeside where he did most of his thinking these days. He tried to remember where he had done most of his thinking in Moscow, then realized that perhaps he had not done as much as he could there. Shaking his head, he walked back from the railing and sat on one of the low benches, still overlooking the great hall. He had practically memorized the reports which littered his desk. The Cubans, always the Cubans.

After the War, Florida had been ceded to them to appease the Communist leader of their island nation. He decided that had been a policy mistake on the part of the Premier and the Politburo. Reports indicated the Communist Cubans had made several incursions into southernmost Georgia—Soviet territory. There were reports of concentration camps, mass executions of Cuban Americans. It was that sort of thing, Varakov knew, that undermined anything positive he could do to relieve the pressure from American Resistance groups. His own command had prisons established to hold captured Resistance personnel and other suspected undesirables; but the camps were humanely run—he checked on them personally. There were few executions, and only those of Resistance people caught in the act of taking a Soviet life. It was, after all, war. The Cubans, he thought. . . . What they reportedly did was not war. There had been two dangerous confrontations between Soviet patrols and Cuban forces in southern Georgia already. Doubtlessly there would be more, he knew.

"Castro," Varakov muttered.

It was clear, he felt, that something had to be done with the Cubans—and quickly. He had no desire for "border" conflicts over something he considered as useless as Florida. And his assessments over the years of the Communist Cuban regime had always led to what he felt was an inescapable conclusion—it was immature. With persons who behaved as irresponsible juvenile delinquents, he decided, one could never be too cautious.

After sifting through the reports, he had spent an almost equal amount of time perusing personnel files. He rubbed his hands together, standing on his sore feet and walking back toward the railing, his uniform jacket unbuttoned. Varakov wiggled his toes inside his shoes, staring down into the main hall. Col. Constantine Miklov was the perfect man—a senior officer and a prudent individual, experienced in dealing with the Cubans after three years as a military adviser there. Miklov's Spanish, Varakov understood from the file, was faultless.

A smile crossed Varakov's lips. In the one area where Miklov was slightly lacking—intelligence background—Varakov could compensate and at the same time achieve an ancillary goal. Natalia Tiemerovna. He had recently promoted her to major. Almost fully recovered from the beating Vladmir Karamatsov—her now-dead husband thanks to the American Rourke—had administered to her, she was wanting an assignment. She spoke Spanish well, Varakov knew, and her natural frankness—the quality that so much endeared her to him—made her more important and more valuable than her relationship to him as his niece. All this would make it easier for her to discover what rationale were behind the Cuban incursions into Soviet occupied territory.

He leaned against the railing, amused at his own thinking. Was he really sending her because of his needs, or because he saw a need in her that this would fulfill?

He shrugged the problem away, thinking that perhaps of late he had become more of an uncle and less of a general in matters concerning Natalia. He should have engineered things to have Rourke killed, he knew, following the assassination of Karamatsov. But Rourke had not really assassinated the man— afterwards it had appeared there had been a "fair" fight between them, Rourke winning. Varakov shrugged again—he liked Rourke. A good man was a good man, Varakov thought, despite his politics. He smiled, then—whether Natalia admitted it to herself or not, and despite her vow to kill Rourke after learning he had killed her husband, the incredibly beautiful Natalia loved the wild and deadly American.

Varakov began to laugh out loud, turning from the balcony railing and starting down the long, low stairs back toward the main hall and his adjoining office. It amused him that he was so concerned over a potentially volatile situation between Russia and Cuba. "I should be more concerned about that," he muttered as he reached the base of the stairs, wondering what he would do if something were to happen that brought Natalia and Rourke together— the KGB major and the ex-C.I.A. covert operations officer.

"Amusing," he said, passing his tall, young secretary, then chuckling again as it seemed evident her eyes were trying to decipher his laughter. "Nothing," he told her good-naturedly, walking toward his desk. Then under his breath he muttered, "Nothing yet."

Chapter 7

"Who is it?"

"If they're close enough to answer, it's usually too late to shoot," John Rourke said, stepping out of the shadows of the small stand of pines, less than six feet from the reddish-brown-haired woman, her hair almost black in the twilight.

"My God—do you always—"

"No, I don't usually creep up on people—just wanted to make certain you were alone," Rourke told her, taking two steps and standing beside her as she sat on the ground, her back propped against some rocks. "How are you feeling, Sissy?" he asked, bending down beside her, studying her face despite the shadows.

"Tired, nervous—better though, I think," she said. "Here—take this back." She handed Rourke the Metalifed two-inch Colt Lawman .357 he'd left with her earlier. "Guns make me nervous."

"No reason guns should do anything to you," he told

her, his voice low. "A gun is just like a screwdriver, a saw, a stethescope, a scalpel—or a seismograph," Rourke added.

"You can't kill someone with a seismograph, though," the girl said, her voice tired.

Lighting one of the small cigars with the Zippo, then clicking the lighter shut and studying it in his left hand, Rourke inhaled hard, exhaling and watching as the gray smoke trailed up into the dim sunlight above the level of the rocks. "You can misuse anything, or you can use it for good—guns aren't any different. I could take one of these—" and he opened his coat, patting the butt of the stainless Detonics under his left arm—"and go become a Brigand like those people chasing you this morning. Or, do what I did—fight the Brigands. I can use the gun for either job, can't I? It doesn't change the nature of the gun, the gun itself has no personality, does it?"

"Well, no . . ."

"Guns bother people because the people don't understand them. People are generally afraid of something they don't understand. Try showing a seismograph to an Australian bushman and the stylus moving along the graph paper making strange lines will scare him to death—just like you and this." Rourke balanced the little Colt in his right hand, then slipped it under his jacket in the small of his back.

"Maybe you're right," the girl said. "But—weapons, all of that—it caused this," she said as she stared toward the orange-red horizon.

"No," Rourke whispered. "Just like my analogy with the Brigands. Nuclear power could have been used for good, and in a lot of ways it was—maybe it still will be.

50

It's the same thing with people not understanding something, being afraid of it. The Russians never really understood us; we never really understood them. The few on both sides who did understand didn't start the war. It was the people who never took the time to understand, or the ones who didn't want to. That's why you're trying to alert what's left of Army Intelligence to an impending disaster; that's why I'm searching for my wife and children. Not enough people understood or cared to. That's why we're here now."

"It's all over, really—isn't it?" the girl whispered hoarsely, her words choked and halting.

"I think so—I'm not sure. I don't know if anybody is. But you can't just lie down and die. As long as you're breathing there's a chance."

"But the sunsets, the sunrises, the weather—all of it—" the woman began.

"We've done something that may never have been done before, or maybe the world reached a level of sophistication like ours eons ago—I don't know," he whispered slowly. "Maybe history does repeat itself. All the crap we belted into the atmosphere—it hasn't been like that since there was mass vulcanism millions of years ago. What kind of effect it's going to have, I don't know. I'm a doctor—you're a scientist. Do you know?"

"No, but . . ."

"Maybe you're lucky—maybe we're both lucky."

Rourke looked up at the sky again. The sun had finally winked below the horizon and stars were visible, though the sky seemed purple more than black or deep blue.

"Do you think there's anyone out there?" she asked,

her voice soft, little-girl sounding.

"Maybe that's the greatest tragedy of this whole thing," Rourke answered slowly. "Maybe we'll never know. I kind of think there has to be. Maybe if we'd encountered a civilization that had gotten itself over the technological hump and still survived we could have learned how to do it."

"You're a strange man, John—I mean, a doctor who runs around on a motorcycle and carries guns. You don't fit any mold I ever encountered."

"I'll take that as a compliment." Rourke smiled in the darkness. "We'd better get on the way to Savannah—see what we can do to contact what government there is."

"Then you got the gas for your motorcycle?"

"Uh-huh," Rourke answered absently. He stared starward—wondering.

Chapter 8

"I think I'm the last—Jeez! That hurts!"

Sarah Rourke bent over the blond-haired man's left thigh, her face close to it. The wound didn't smell and she surmised that was a good sign. She wished she'd taken her hospital volunteer work more seriously, or watched John more closely the few times she'd seen him work. She remembered once shortly after they'd married they had met a doctor Rourke had worked with during his internship, before he'd essentially abandoned medicine and gone to work for the Central Intelligence Agency. The man—she tried to remember his name . . . Feinstein? Feinburg? It was something like that, she'd decided. The man, whatever his name, had told her something while John had stepped away for a few moments. John still smoked cigarettes in those days, and he might have gone to get a fresh pack. It was years ago, she thought. The doctor had told her, though, that John had been the most promising man he'd ever worked with in medicine—with hands skilled enough to make him a top surgeon, had he chosen to become one, and a mind quick enough to make important life-and-death decisions and then act. The latter quality—the doctor's name had been Feinmann, she finally remembered—was the rare thing, the thing that made greatness in a doctor.

Sarah Rourke looked at the Resistance fighter on the cot beside her. "What's your name?" she remembered to ask.

"Harmon Kleinschmidt," he told her, the voice strained.

"Well, Mr. Klein—" She stopped and started again. "Harmon—my husband, the childrens' father, is a doctor. I'm not. I had some first-aid courses, rolled bandages as a volunteer, and watched my husband operate a few times in emergencies. I know what to do to get your wounds cleaned up, maybe I can even take out a bullet if it isn't too close to something vital. But since I'm the best you've got right now and since we've got Russians all around us, why don't you just shut up and bite on a towel or something and let me do what I can. Okay?"

Kleinschmidt fell back against the rolled blanket he used as a pillow. "Can I talk?" he rasped. She didn't look up at him, but it sounded as though he'd spoken through clenched teeth.

"Sure—if it helps," she whispered. She glanced over her shoulder. Michael and Annie were rubbing down the horses, not watching. She was happy for that because the leg wound wasn't pretty, and after that there was still the shoulder wound.

"They got all of us—all but me. Most of the women

and kids pulled out after the men all got themselves nailed. Me, I tried making it somewhere, anywhere—I wound up here."

Sarah didn't think the man was making too much sense, "What happened?" she asked, not really caring, but trying to keep his mind occupied. There was a big, deformed chunk of metal very close to the bone in his upper thigh and she knew that removing it would hurt.

"Well . . . hmmm," he groaned. "Well, they—the Reds—we figured to git 'em. Figured they needed Savannah as a seaport. Rumors seem to be the Ruskies gave Florida over to Castro's army. If they couldn't use Florida, Savannah would have to have been mighty important as a seaport. So, we figured we could screw 'em good—sorry ma'am," he rasped, "if we made their lives miserable. We were doin' okay 'til we started coordinating everythin' with that U.S. II."

"What's U.S. II?" Sarah asked. She was using a small pair of forceps from the first-aid kit John had made up before the Night of the War and she had carried it from the house. "The house," she groaned under her breath.

"What ma'am?" Kleinschmidt asked.

"Nothing, Harmon. Tell me what U.S. II is? Go on." She started probing with the forceps for the bullet. Any minute now, he'd scream, she told herself.

"Well, I don't completely understand it myself. Seems some fella named Sam Chambers was the last man to survive from the President's cabinet. Makes him the new President. There was a letter goin' 'round—some guys had it. My friend Jock Whitman read a copy of it—the President, the real one, he killed himself so the Commies couldn't make him surrender."

"I didn't know that. Are you sure?" she asked him.

55

"Yeah—well, the letter said that, Jock told me. There was supposed to be copies of it all over what's left of the country. Story was the Secret Service got it out for him. When we started working with U.S. II, they said the same thing. But there's gotta be some kind of problem with them. After we started coordinating everythin' with them, the Russians almost seemed to know what we was up to before we did. Some of us figured they had themselves—in U.S. II, that is—some kind of a—aagh!"

She looked up. His body twitched violently and now his eyes were closed, his mouth contorted in pain. But his chest was still rising and falling. As she started to grasp the bullet—at least she assumed it was that—in the forceps, the body twitched again.

"Michael!" she called. "Come hold Mr. Kleinschmidt so he doesn't move when I do this. Annie, stay with the horses."

Michael was beside her in a moment. "Don't look, son," she told him.

"It's all right, Momma," the boy said quietly. Even the voice, his way of speaking, reminded her more and more of John.

"Traitor," she said, pulling the bullet from where it was lodged. She thought it had been imbedded in a muscle but wasn't sure.

"What?"

She looked up at Michael, forcing a smile. "No—not you, never you," she whispered.

"Mr. Kleinschmidt had been talking before he passed out. He was telling me he thought someone was telling the Russians what he and the rest of the Resistance people were doing. You know—like Mary

Mulliner's husband and son. They were in the Resistance. Well," she went on, probing the wound to check if the bullet had left any fragments, "he thought there was a traitor."

There weren't any fragments, and she studied the bloody chunk of metal in the forceps for a moment. It was obviously deformed, but it looked to be in one piece. "Such a little thing," she said, turning it so it would better catch the light.

Sarah Rourke looked at Harmon Kleinschmidt's face. It seemed more peaceful now. She imagined that when he was all cleaned up he probably looked handsome. He'd told her earlier that if she helped him, he knew of a boat they could steal to get them all to safety on one of the offshore islands. Safety, she thought. Then she looked again at the bullet, almost laughing.

Chapter 9

Rourke looked at the woman, his eyes squinted against the sunlight. "You'll be safer here, so relax. It should take me about an hour to get into Savannah on foot. Then once I find my contact I might be able to snitch some transportation to get back faster."

"But why aren't you taking your guns? What will you do if—"

Rourke cut her off. "If I get spotted with a gun, I'm automatically nailed. Soviet-held cities don't even allow Americans to carry pocket knives, let alone firearms. You should like it," Rourke added. "It's total gun control."

"Yes," she began, "but this is different."

"Tell me about it sometime," Rourke said, not particularly caring for her ethical two-facedness. He started walking, the cowboy boots from his pack feeling unfamiliar after all the time he'd been spending wearing combat boots. The brim of the grayish-tan

Stetson Canyon was pulled low over his face against the sun, despite the dark glasses he wore. He'd unintentionally lied to the woman, he thought as he started down from the low rise where he'd left her. He wasn't completely weaponless. The heavy trophy buckle on the belt that held up his Levis made a good weapon in a pinch, there were his hands, too, he reasoned. Rourke's spine shivered slightly—without a gun he felt naked, but perhaps that was the best way.

There was always the disturbing possibility the woman would lose her nerve, steal the bike and the guns, and be gone when he returned. He could always steal a bike himself, he thought, reviewing the possibilities. He'd miss the big customized Harley, though. The other Harley, the one he'd taken from a Brigand he'd killed back in New Mexico after the marauders had slaughtered the survivors of the crashed 747—that Harley was at the Retreat now and he supposed he could work it over to come close to the Low Rider he'd left with Sissy. If he had to.

The guns would be the biggest problem, Rourke decided, leaving the high ground and paralleling a two-lane palm-lined highway leading into the city of Savannah. The twin Detonics stainless .45s would be impossible to replace, as would be the Python and the CAR-15. There was a standard AR-15 at the Retreat, his Metalifed Colt Government .45 was there too. For a revolver he could always use the Metalifed Custom .357 Magnum, the heavily modified three-inch K-Frame with his name engraved on the flatted heavy barrel. It was a superlative gun but still a K-Frame, and high-performance .357 Magnum ammo was not its best diet. He'd used the round-butted Smith & Wesson several times with superior results as a concealment gun. He supposed it would fill the bill now.

He stopped, surveying the road some distance beyond the defile through which he walked, smiling. Likely the woman would be there when he returned; and the guns and the Harley would be in good order. But the mental debate he'd had with himself had passed the miles. In the distance now, he could see the outskirts of Savannah.

Chapter 10

Sarah Rourke had ridden Tildie as close to Savannah as she had dared, leaving Michael in charge of the weak, yet conscious, Harmon Kleinschmidt—as well as Annie. Kleinschmidt had insisted that if she reached Savannah and found the boat he'd spoken of, she could take it and get them all to one of the offshore islands where he could recuperate and she could rest with the children. Sarah had agreed to try.

She'd left her rifle with Kleinschmidt, just taking the .45 automatic in Tildie's saddlebags. She judged it to be an hour's walk when she'd unsaddled Tildie and left her in a clearing, no fear the animal would bolt and run off. She had stored the saddle and the rest of the tack in a wooded area not far from the clearing, then changed clothes, thinking she'd draw less attention to herself if she didn't look as if she'd just come in off the trail. As she walked down the grassy hill now, she could feel the taller grass against her bare legs beneath the hem of the wrap-around denim skirt she wore—a gift from Mary Mulliner who'd gotten it one Christmas from her husband and never worn it. She'd taken a light blue T-shirt that didn't have holes in it yet and worn that; and she even wore a bra for the first time since leaving the Mulliner farm. She hadn't been able to wash her hair, but it was long enough to put up now and she'd done that—hoping for the best.

She reached the road and could see the city ahead. Feeling oddly nervous without her gun, she smiled. "My gun," she whispered, thinking that before the War she would barely touch one and since the War she carried one in the waistband of her pants and slept with it at night. Shaking her head, feeling herself smiling, she started down the road into Savannah, toward the docks where Harmon Kleinschmidt had told her the boat was secured.

Chapter 11

Rourke lit one of the small, dark tobacco cigars. He'd seen a few other men smoking and had decided it wouldn't draw undue attention to himself. But he'd left the Zippo lighter along with his guns and the motorcycle. It stood to reason, he'd decided. Cigarette lighters, which required fuel, would be in disuse generally—no one but the Russians and a few select, important Americans working with them had fuel. He used a stick match instead, cupping his hands around the flame in the slight wind as he stood at the far end of the rough wooden pier, staring down its length toward a decent-sized fishing boat moored there. The name on the boat was *Stargazer II*—it was the name he recalled from the memorized list originally given Paul Rubenstein by Captain Reed. The captain of *Stargazer II* was supposed to be Cal Summers, the local Army Intelligence contact. Rourke hoped that hadn't changed. He tossed down the match and started walking along the dock, the cowboy hat pulled low over his eyes.

There was a man working on the deck. It was early enough that the fishermen of the area hadn't all left yet, and Rourke understood the fuel situation was such that not all boats were allowed out of port each day. Fishing in the surviving coastal towns, Rourke had been told by Reed and confirmed through casual conversation with others he had met, was a vital industry—given another year, the average American survivor of the Night of the War would be starving to death. When the Russians had bombed the center of the country into a nuclear desert, they had also destroyed much of America's prime growing areas. The loss of California and the Imperial Valley's fruit and vegetable crops had been an added disaster. Florida had been so heavily bombed that very little could be grown there. Rourke shook his head. With famine would come even more violence.

He stopped on the pier just behind the aft section of *Stargazer II.* There was a man standing under the canopy, working near the controls. "Excuse me," Rourke shouted over to him.

"What'd you do?" the man answered without looking around.

Rourke smiled, hunching his shoulders against the gathering wind. Without his leather coat, the cowboy shirt he wore suddenly felt inadequate. "I'm coming aboard. You Captain Cal Summers?" Rourke asked, stepping down from the pier and into the boat.

The man turned around, and as he did Rourke's eyes drifted to the man's belt line. There was no bulge, but the sweater had pulled up slightly as the man moved.

"Git off my boat, fella," the man in the sweater stated flatly.

"If you're Cal Summers, we've got business," Rourke went on, his voice low, even.

"I'm Cal Summers, but I ain't got no business with you, fella. Now go on—git!"

Rourke took a step forward, glancing over his shoulder, leading with his right hand, certain no one was watching. As the man in the sweater started to move, Rourke's left hand reached out, scooping at the butt of the gun under the sweater.

The gun was in his hand as Cal Summers started to react, but Rourke had already dodged, moving back toward the stern of the boat.

Rourke held the gun close in front of him, saying half to himself, "Smith & Wesson 66 2½, with a Barami Hip Grip—not bad."

Cal Summers took a step toward him and Rourke raised the muzzle of the stubby-barreled stainless steel revolver. Summers stopped. Rourke glanced over his shoulder, making certain again that no one was watching, then over-ended the gun in his left hand, not really making a full spin. He reached the gun out for Summers to take the black butt.

Summers, his eyes shifting from right to left, snatched the gun and rammed it into his waistband, under his sweater. "What the hell you want? Who are you?"

"Let's go inside," Rourke told him. "Not out here."

"Below deck then," the man said, his eyes wary.

Cal Summers started below first, and Rourke, glancing left, then right, followed him down.

Chapter 12

Sarah Rourke stopped, a gust of wind catching at her
skirt, her body cold in the sudden chill. She looked
down along the pier. At the far end she could see the
name Kleinschmidt had told her to look for—the *Ave
Maria*. It looked awfully big to her, but she walked
along the pier, determined to see it up close anyway.
There were many boats, looking to belong to fishermen, ranked one beside the other; only a few of the
slots along the pier were empty. Few of the craft
showed anyone near them.

She stopped again, staring—a shiver coursing up her
spine, but not from the cold. It had been the cowboy
hat she decided. John had worn one just like that
sometimes. She wondered what a man wearing a
tannish-gray Stetson was doing going down into a
fishing boat. There was something about the set of the
shoulders as the man had moved his head quickly after
glancing over his right shoulder, a familiarity as he had

stood there a moment peering down into the cabin.

"Eerie," she muttered, then walked on, past the boat. She glanced at the name, the tall man with the cowboy hat below deck now. The boat was called *Stargazer II*. As she walked on, toward the huge craft at the end of the pier, *Ave Maria,* she glanced over her shoulder toward the *Stargazer II*. But the man who'd reminded her for an instant of John Rourke was nowhere in sight.

Chapter 13

Rourke searched for a butt can or ashtray, found neither and flicked the ashes from the small cigar into his left palm.

"Now, who the hell are you?" Cal Summers leaned against the far bulkhead by the forward section of the below-deck cabin, his right hand close to the front of his pants—close to the stainless .357 Magnum under his sweater.

"My name's John Rourke. Army Intelligence gave me your name, name of the boat."

"Which army?" Summers snapped.

"Ours—or what's left of it," Rourke answered softly. "Captain Reed—know him?"

"Yeah. How do I know you do?"

"Well," Rourke said thoughtfully, "if I were a Russian, you'd have already hanged yourself."

"Bullshit—you'd be wantin' to get next to me to find

out where the rest of the Resistance people are holed up."

"How close you keep in touch with U.S. II?" Rourke queried.

"None of your damned business."

Rourke smiled. "You hear about the deal when Chambers got nabbed by the Russians?"

"Maybe," Summers grunted.

"Well, hear about a guy who busted him out?"

"There was another fella with him," Summers admitted.

"Yeah, but Paul Rubenstein's down in Florida, trying to see if his parents made it through the War or not."

"Anybody can learn names," Summers snapped.

"What do you want, then?" Rourke asked.

"There was somethin' peculiar about the guy's gun," Summers began. "At least that's what I heard."

Rourke smiled. "Well, I don't know who you heard it from, but I imagine you mean 'guns' rather than gun." Summers's expression began to soften. "I usually carry a matched pair of Stainless Detonics .45s—left 'em back with the rest of my gear, just outside of town. That what you're lookin' for?" Rourke smiled again.

"Sorry," Summers said, taking a few steps forward across the cabin and stretching out his right hand. Rourke shook it, then Summers stepped back. "Here— I got an old butt can around here somewhere." He disappeared into what Rourke guessed was the galley, then reappeared a moment later. There was a small, round plastic ashtray in his left hand and he reached it onto the flat railing beside Rourke.

Nodding, Rourke asked, "Aren't you a little reckless with that gun? People could see it."

"Gotta be," Summers agreed. "See, the Communists nailed most of the Resistance people—maybe a couple got away. Their wives, girl friends, sisters, whatever—all the women and the kids are on one of the offshore islands. I try smugglin' out food 'and some medical stuff when I can. But the Communists could find me out any time. You might wanna get out of here, yourself. I figure I'll go down shootin' rather than wind up with the KGB skinnin' me alive or somethin'—I heard about them when I was R.A. years back."

"So, what?" Rourke asked. "You were Regular Army, got in the reserve or something, then after the Night of the War they called you up. How?"

"I got tied in with the Resistance—that Captain Reed and some sergeant hunted me out here after I'd already sort of volunteered through the Resistance. Reed brought me a radio, in case I needed to contact him. Shouldn't have took it," Summers said soberly.

"Why?" Rourke asked.

"Well, there's some kind of traitor—gotta be—in U.S. II. The Resistance had a big raid planned last Friday night."

"What the hell day is it today?" Rourke asked.

"Thursday."

"Yeah—what happened?"

"I radioed in, used a code Reed said the Reds didn't have. Then when the raid came off, the Reds was there—jumped the Resistance guys, killed some, arrested the others. Got 'em in an old textile plant, and they're usin' it as a prison. Best I can learn, they ain't exactly makin' 'em feel like it's a big hotel or nothin', but they're feedin' and lookin' after 'em—they're executin' some of them too. I guess they gotta, to be fair to 'em. Maybe we'd do the same with a Resistance movement. They do what they gotta do; we do what we gotta do, I figure. Some damned silly game gettin' people killed. Wish we could cream all them Reds and send the ones left packin' to Moscow. Someday, you think?"

"All we can do is try," Rourke commented non-committally. "But I've got a more immediate problem. You don't think they cracked your code do you?"

"I was in Intelligence for ten years before I decided not to re-up, then with the Reserve until the War. They didn't crack this code—I'd guarantee it."

"Is the radio safe then?" Rourke asked.

"That why you come to see me?"

"Well, yeah," Rourke admitted. "I picked up a woman yesterday morning. She's a scientist. She discovered something with a bunch of the people she worked with, and we've gotta let U.S. II know about it right away. That's why I came here. Figured a radio was the fastest way of getting the information out."

"If you gotta. But I don't trust them people back there in U.S. II—some kind of Red-nosed rat is in with 'em if you get my drift."

"I get your drift, but I've got no choice," Rourke told Summers flatly. "Where's the radio?"

"Help me cast off. Hope you can swim, too—that water's too cold for me these days."

Rourke eyed the man, nodding. Pulling the Stetson back low over his eyes, he started up on deck. Rourke stood there, feeling the wind on his face, smelling the salt-scented air over the water. As Rourke followed

Summers's lead and began casting off, he looked up the length of the pier. There was a woman—odd he thought—staring at a large fishing boat, larger by far than any of the others. Rourke squinted against the light. It looked to him as though the name were *Ave Maria*. He looked at the woman as he coiled in the line. The wind was blowing up the back of the blue denim skirt she wore. She had pretty legs, he thought; and for a moment she reminded him of Sarah. Shaking his head slowly as the woman walked out of sight beyond some bales at the end of the pier, he snapped the cigar butt into the water.

Whatever happened with the predicted quake along the new fault line in Florida, he wanted the thing resolved. He wondered how much time there was left to find Sarah and the children. The wind was blowing harder and Rourke tugged the brim of the Stetson down lower over his eyes.

Chapter 14

Sarah Rourke leaned against the bales at the edge of the pier, hugging her arms close about her against the cold wind that whipped at her hair and at her legs beneath the skirt. She looked at the *Ave Maria*. "Too big," she whispered to herself.

She couldn't envision Harmon Kleinschmidt being well enough to steer the boat away from the pier for at least a week or perhaps longer. Michael could help her cast off, but the only boats she had ever operated had been small outboards. Once she had driven a slightly larger boat when John had been waterskiing. She shook her head, telling herself she couldn't handle it. She would have to steal something, something smaller. She started back along the pier, noticing the *Stargazer II* that had attracted her attention earlier. There was a man wearing a sweater and a knit watchcap at the wheel, the boat pulling away from the pier. There was no sign of anyone else.

The boat next to the *Stargazer II*'s berth looked about the right size, but she wondered how you stole a boat. Shrugging, she walked more quickly, hugging her arms to her chest, the cold wind lashing against her bare arms and legs.

"What would John do?" she asked herself—a question she'd been asking herself ever since the Night of the War.

Chapter 15

Wearing a borrowed windbreaker, his hat below deck, Rourke joined Cal Summers at the wheel of the fishing boat. "How far out are we going?" Rourke shouted over the wind and the engine noise.

"Far as we want. Ain't no where to go in the world really, so the Ruskies don't care much if we leave—but it's only a couple more miles. I didn't want to get caught with a radio—Russians took 'em all off the boats before they let us use 'em again. So, I packed the radio in a waterproof container, then swam down and stowed it under some rocks. It's a good swim, but it ain't too deep along here yet. I had this fella Harmon Kleinschmidt who worked with me a while do most of the divin' every time we needed the radio. Harmon might have got killed durin' that Resistance roundup—I ain't sure. Best I can learn, he ain't in prison, though. You swim, right?"

Rourke nodded, not smiling. The water, he thought,

would have to be warmer than the air.

After another fifteen minutes, Rourke noticed the boat slowing. He returned from the stern to stand beside Cal Summers again. "You got any diving equipment?"

"Nope. Russians took it. Figured diving gear could be used to plant mines or somethin'. You won't need none—if you can hold your breath good."

"Wonderful!" Rourke shouted over the wind, the engine noise subsiding as the boat slowed, moving almost imperceptibly forward now, swaying with the waves that the wind whipped up against them.

Rourke began to strip away the borrowed windbreaker, watching Summers checking a compass. A smile crossed the sweater-clad, older man's face, his blue eyes brightening. "Dead over her—pretty good. Hell, I shoulda been in the Navy, not no Army!"

Rourke laughed, shivering already as he tugged open the snaps on the front of the dark brown western-cut shirt he wore.

Leaning against the portside railing, Rourke pulled off his cowboy boots, then skinned out of his Levis, then his socks.

"Want me to hold your watch for you?"

Rourke looked at Summers, then grinned. "It's a Rolex—more waterproof than this boat. Thanks anyway."

Rourke stood by the rail, Summers pointing out about six feet away from the hull. "There and straight down," he said.

"Same to you," Rourke muttered with a grin, swinging his left leg over the portside rail, then his right. He perched there on the rail a moment, then added, "And if the Russians come or something, let me know." Without waiting for an answer, Rourke pushed himself off with his feet, diving out into the water, the wind and the water temperature chilling him so badly that he began to shake with the cold.

He glanced up at the fishing boat, Summers giving him a quick salute, then Rourke tucked down, under the water, his mouth closing as he broke the surface. His lungs already felt it as he swam downward. At least a weight belt would have been useful, Rourke thought. The water was reasonably clean and he could already see the sandy bottom. That the water was so clear indicated nothing had disturbed the bottom recently. Rourke made a mental note to check himself with the Geiger counter in case the ocean here was radioactive— but he doubted the Russians would have allowed fishing if it were. And he was almost certain they periodically checked. It was only common sense, Rourke reasoned.

His arms fanned away from his sides, and Rourke's feet touched bottom. Immediately the sand and silt there stirred up in a cloud from his disturbing it. He could see the mound of rocks there which Cal Summers had described, then moved along the bottom the few feet remaining to reach them. Had Summers not described it, Rourke thought, he would have spotted something strange at any event. The clouds of silt increased in density as Rourke reached the rocks. Then he pried the top, flat rock away, letting it bounce to the bottom beside the pile, a large amount of the sand and silt now clouding the water.

Rourke waved his left hand in front of him, as one might do it in the air to clear away a smoke cloud.

77

There, inside the cup of rocks, was a waterproof container. A small fish Rourke couldn't instantly identify swayed past it as he reached down, carefully prying at the radio lest some small sea creature had decided to use the rock nest as a home—some small sea creature that could bite or stick.

In the water, the weight of the object seemed off to him, but he assumed it was the radio. The water-proof packing seemed to have kept its integrity. Leaving the capping rock where it had dropped, the radio under his left arm, Rourke pushed himself up with his knees and feet and started clawing toward the surface. He glanced awkwardly at the Rolex—he had been down better than two minutes and the burning feeling in his lungs told him his time was running out.

He could see the light shimmering from the surface as he reached out toward it, the radio suddenly feeling heavier to him. His hand broke the water above him, then his head. Rourke opened his mouth, exhaling hard and sucking in air with his mouth and nose. Scanning from side to side, he saw the boat—he'd come up on the starboard side.

To be on the careful side, he thought, he didn't shout to Summers. He swam instead the dozen or so feet toward the fishing boat. There was a small ladder over the side and, clinging to the bottom rung, balancing the edge of the radio against it, Rourke shifted his grip quickly, two rungs up, hauling his right foot to the bottom rung, still holding the radio. Balanced there, Rourke peered over the side, into the fishing boat. He could see Summers, standing there looking out to port. A smile crossed Rourke's lips as he watched the man. "Captain," he said, his voice low.

Summers wheeled, the gun coming into his right hand, his face twisted into something Rourke thought seemed half between a snarl and a look of surprise.

"God, man! You scared ten years out of me!" Summers shoved the revolver back in his trousers and started across the deck.

Rourke said, "Just being on the safe side. Now help me with this blasted radio!"

Chapter 16

Varakov sat at his desk, slipping his shoes off. He smiled, looking first at his niece Natalia, then at Constantine Miklov, then back at Natalia. "You are lovely, my dear—as usual, of course," he told her.

The girl smiled, saying nothing.

Varakov said nothing for a moment either, assessing her. She was dressed in black, as she had been since learning of the death of Karamatsov, but she looked beautiful in black and Varakov decided he would rather see her wear a black dress every day for the rest of her life than think of her with the animal she had married.

Her dark hair flowed to her shoulders and beyond, and with the contrasting bright blue of her eyes, the whiteness of her skin seemed somehow unreal, almost too perfect. In that instant, Varakov decided he understood why Karamatsov had beaten her—though he could never forgive it in the man, despite the fact

Karamatsov was dead.

Karamatsov had somehow wanted to defile the perfection, the goddess-like beauty. It could have been hard, Varakov decided, for a man like Karamatsov—a despoiler, what the British before World War II in their days of empire would have called a "rotter"—to live with flawless beauty such as Natalia possessed. He sighed, watching the girl's eyes meet his.

He smiled at her, saying to her across his desk, "An old man sometimes finds his thoughts drifting to other things. It is part of life."

Varakov turned to Colonel Miklov, beginning, "You were briefed on the Cuban problem, the border incursions from Florida, all of that?"

Miklov nodded. Varakov liked that in Miklov. He said little.

"Good—Natalia will be there officially in the capacity of an aide. If they realize she is KGB, then they do. They can do nothing to either of you. We would crush them and they know that."

Then Varakov turned to Natalia. "And you, my dear. It is not such a unique intelligence assignment. I simply wish you to learn all that you can, especially that which they do not wish you to know. If they suspect you are KGB, they will feed you information on their strength, their intentions—all of that. That is why I chose you particularly for this assignment. I need all this to be seen through, so to speak. I wish to ascertain their actual intent, their actual strength."

"How far should I go, Comrade General?" she asked, the warmth in her eyes belying the formality of her tone.

Varakov smiled, saying, "That is entirely up to your

own discretion."

"I don't mean that," she almost laughed, her cheeks slightly flushed.

"I know what you mean. Do what needs to be done," he told her. "So long as it does not immediately result in you or Colonel Miklov being imperiled. Neither the Colonel's diplomatic negotiations nor what you learn, by whatever means, will be of any use if you should be killed in some unfortunate accident. You understand?"

"Yes, Comrade General."

"Good," Varakov grunted. He glanced at the notes he'd made, then turned and addressed Miklov. The meeting lasted for more than an hour, Varakov noted. Miklov and Natalia Tiemerovna were set to leave early that evening from the military airfield northwest of the city. Varakov asked if Miklow would care for a glass of vodka, but Miklov declined, Varakov dismissing him then. It was late afternoon and Varakov decided he had worked enough that day. Sitting silently with Natalia across from him, Varakov looked up from his desk, saying abruptly, "Would you walk with me along the Lake. It is cold, I know, but—"

"Yes, Uncle," he said, her voice soft sounding to him.

"Good—I want to talk. There are so few people to whom one can talk these days," he told her.

The general slipped his feet into his shoes, then wheeled out from his desk and bent over to tie them. Suddenly he looked up at Natalia standing beside him. "Here, Uncle—let me." And before he could tell her no, she had dropped to her knees beside his feet, her hands already at work.

"I am not a child," he said, but his voice not harsh.

She looked up at him a faint smile on her lips. "A

woman can tie a man's shoes. It means nothing like that."

"Humph," he grunted, but didn't persist.

"There," she said, rising effortlessly to her feet. Varakov looked down at his shoes, simply shaking his head, then braced his left hand on the desk top and got to his feet.

"Girl!" he shouted, never seeming, he thought, to remember the name of the tall woman who was his secretary. But she came whatever he called her.

"Comrade General!"

Varakov looked at the secretary, then at Natalia. Their ages were similar—late twenties. He supposed that under their clothes their shapes might be similar. He was too old, he smiled, to worry about that.

"Child," he told the secretary, more softly. "I need my coat, please."

"Yes, Comrade General." And the woman did a smart about face.

He called after her, the woman stopping a moment in mid-stride. "Your skirt is still too long!" She began walking again.

Varakov looked at Natalia, her cheeks slightly flushed. "Isn't it?" he asked his niece.

"Yes, Uncle—but you embarrass her. It is not my position to say, but I—"

"When you get back from this Florida thing, you tell her, hmmm?"

"As you wish, Uncle," Natalia said, the color still in her cheeks.

They left the Museum then. Natalia, Varakov noticed, smiled at the secretary as she brought his coat. They walked down the steps, then toward what had been Lake Shore Drive. There was scattered military traffic, but they crossed easily, the sun low behind them, the wind blowing cold from the water ahead of them.

"It is too cold for you, Natalia?" Varakov asked her.

"No, Uncle." And he watched as she seemed to draw herself into the mid-calf length, almost black fur coat.

He took her right elbow in his left hand, guiding her along the comparatively narrow peninsula on a sidewalk toward the lake itself. "Is that coat real fur?"

"Yes, Uncle," she answered, her voice sounding odd to him. He guessed she was cold but too polite to say it.

"You are not uncomfortable—it is not too cold here?"

"No, I am comfortable," she answered.

"A lot of money?"

"What, Uncle?"

"The coat, I mean."

"Yes."

"Is it easier now?"

"What is that?"

"The passing of your husband, I mean. I should ask. It is perhaps a source of anguish to you still. I am sure, in fact, that it is," he said, turning to her. "You are crying?"

He studied her blue eyes. "It is the wind, Uncle," she answered.

He could see the lake waters ahead—choppy, he thought. "I see. But is it any easier?"

He stopped walking. He gazed down to see the waves surround the rocky peninsula, hammering at it as the wind whipped them. Then he turned again to Natalia.

The tears were still in her eyes.

"No. Rourke killed him. He promised he wouldn't, then he murdered him. No!"

"Would you—do you love Rourke, still?" Varakov asked her. "Would you kill Rourke for what he did?"

"Yes," she said, the tears stopping in her eyes a moment. He studied her face. "I love him, but I would kill him. He had no right, no reason to—"

The wind was audible now, howling. Varakov interrupted her, saying, "No right, no reason. . . . He may have saved your life, this man Rourke. Karamatsov was an animal. You know this thing. I know this thing. Who knows, perhaps Rourke saw this too."

"It was deliberate, Uncle—like the gunfight he had just before the helicopters found us in the rain, there in the desert. I told you—we joined the Brigands only to save the lives of the townspeople they were going to kill. Rourke fought the Brigand leader and two of his men. Then he fought one more man with guns—and killed the man. At the time, I felt Rourke was insane. But—" and she turned away. With the wind Varakov could barely hear her. "I was happy when Rourke survived."

"Natalia—" Varakov began.

The girl turned, facing him—no longer, he thought, hiding the tears in her eyes. "He fought Vladmir like that, killed him like that Brigand."

"You told me once that Brigand had done some horrible thing. What was it?"

"I don't remember," she said.

"You remember—he had killed a woman's infant child, yes?"

"Yes," she answered, her voice low again.

"Why do you think Rourke killed Vladmir Karamatsov?"

"I don't know."

"Jealousy—to get you?"

"No—not jealousy, not for me," she almost shrieked, looking at him.

"You are right, and you are wrong," Varakov told her. "I would never have told you this thing, but I have watched you these days since it had happened. You eat at yourself, you blame yourself, but you should not. Rourke killed your husband only because I forced him to, to save American Resistance fighters captured with him. I ordered him to assassinate Karamatsov." Varakov watched her face, the eyes widening, the mouth open, the lips parted, the set of her jaw. Her tears had stopped again. "But he apparently would not—so he killed Vladmir in the fairest way he could—in a cowboy-style gunfight from the American western movies. Rourke killed the man because I forced him to do this thing. He pulled the trigger. I pointed the gun," Varakov concluded.

"I cannot, cannot believe you would do this thing."

"Your Rourke—he is smart, he is clever. He could have agreed, then decided to help his comrades escape, never have killed Vladmir. But I told Rourke why—I told him what Karamatsov had done to you, why Karamatsov had to die."

"No!" she screamed, turning, running from him out along the peninsula.

Varakov watched her, shrugging, not attempting to run after her. He hunched his shoulders against the wind, holding the peak of his cap, walking after her. He shouted once, "Natalia!"

The girl did not stop running. He could see her, at the far end of the peninsula, stopped now because there was no further place to run.

It took him several minutes, he judged, to reach the end of the peninsula—by a museum of astronomy. He slowed his pace, his feet hurting, walking up to her. "Natalia Tiemerovna, can you still love your uncle?"

He stopped, six feet or so behind her. The girl turned, her hands coming from the pockets of her fur coat, her arms reaching out as she ran the few steps toward him. She put her arms around his neck. He could no longer see her face. He looked beyond it at the waves, feeling her body against his massive chest and stomach, hearing her sobs below the keening of the wind. "Can you still love your uncle?" he asked again, his voice low, his lips close to her right ear.

"Yes," she murmured.

Varakov smiled. He didn't ask the other question that hung between them. And he knew the answer concerning Rourke, and he feared it.

Chapter 17

Sarah Rourke swung down from Tildie's saddle, her hands sliding across the animal's neck. She started to wipe the lather down along her thighs, but remembered she was still wearing the skirt. She reached up to the blue jeans tied to the saddle thongs and wiped the sweat from her hands. Then she took her pants and reached into the saddlebag for her gun, leading Tildie toward the farmhouse.

She looked from side to side, double-checking as she had since coming in sight of the farmhouse that there were no signs of Soviet troops or Brigands. She stopped at the door, knocking. "Michael, it's momma," she said loudly.

The door opened and she stepped inside, tugging at the reins of the mare behind her, bending and kissing Michael. "Did anything happen?"

"No, nothing. Did you find the boat, Momma?"

She kissed the boy again. "I did, but—"

"Mrs. Rourke, you found the boat?"

She turned around. It was odd not to hear herself addressed as someone's mother. She stared across the room. Harmon Kleinschmidt was sitting up on the cot, his back propped against the wall. "You shouldn't be sitting up, Harmon—not with those wounds," she told him.

"But you found it?"

She looked at Kleinschmidt a moment, turned toward Michael and handed him Tildie's reins, saying, "Michael, rub her down and feed her. I'll need her again soon."

The boy moved off and Sarah Rourke turned again toward Kleinschmidt. Annie was asleep on some blankets on the floor, and Sarah, as she walked across the room, stooped down, kissing the girl's forehead, tucking the blankets up around her. Sarah was still cold from the ride outside in the wind.

"I found your boat, Mr. Kleinschmidt. I saw a lot of boats."

"Did you see the *Stargazer II?* I used to work on it."

"As a matter of fact I did," she told the younger man. "I need a boat that size. Why can't we ask the man who owns it, if you used to work on it?"

She stepped beside the cot, automatically checking the bandages. They didn't need changing yet, she determined.

"I can't risk it for him. They might be watching him anyway, looking for me."

Sarah nodded, saying nothing.

"But you saw the *Ave Maria*—you saw it?"

"You can't operate the boat, Harmon," she told him, looking at him evenly. "And even with the children helping me, I can't operate something that big either. I need a smaller boat, like the *Stargazer II.* I need a place we can leave the horses, then I need a way of getting us to the boat, though. Can you help me there?"

"Yeah, but I just don't see why you don't want the *Ave Maria.* Why?"

Sarah stood up, walking behind a blanket suspended from a rope she'd run across the opposite corner of the house. She hadn't felt like undressing with Harmon Kleinschmidt being able to wake up at any moment and watch her. Behind the blanket, she dug down into one of the duffel bags. There was a pair of pink shorts she remembered that had gotten caught up with her blue jeans when she'd packed hurriedly that first time they'd left the farmhouse in northeast Georgia, right after the bombing. She'd been tempted to throw the shorts away, but kept them in case the weather became hot. She studied the shorts a moment. "Swimsuit," she muttered to herself. Then, starting to undress behind the screening blanket, she said to Kleinschmidt, "What was it you were saying, Harmon?"

"Why not the *Ave Maria*? She's a good ship."

"She's too much of a ship," Sarah said back to him, stripping off the T-shirt, then the bra, then putting them on top of her skirt and her underpants. She pulled on the shorts, then the T-shirt again. "I can't handle it, so if the Russians were after us, I couldn't outrun them," she said finally.

"All right—but you could get the horses on her."

"But I'm not taking the *Ave Maria,* Harmon. That's final." She stepped into her track shoes, bending to tie them, saying, "Michael—carefully—get me that boning knife from the other duffel bag." She let her hair down as she stepped from behind the blanket. The hell with not washing it, she thought—it'd be wet soon enough.

"Momma, why are you wearing shorts? It's cold outside. You wouldn't—"

She cut the boy off. "I don't feel like going for a swim in my blue jeans, Michael."

"A swim, Mrs. Rourke?" Harmon Kleinschmidt asked.

"I asked myself, Harmon, what would my husband do in a situation like this. Well, my husband is very good at things like this—always was. I guess it isn't a secret anymore that he was in the C.I.A., he was a survival expert, and a doctor too. He's alive somewhere. That's what the children and I are doing— looking for him. I tell myself he's looking for us. I know he is," she automatically corrected herself. "If John were doing this—that's my husband—well, he'd go back to the pier at night, go into the water, swim up alongside one of the boats and steal it. He'd take a knife," she said and raised the boning knife to show Kleinschmidt as Michael handed it to her. "And, I guess he'd use it if he had to," she added.

"I can't let you do that, Mrs. Rourke."

"I feel old enough these days, Harmon. Just call me Sarah," she smiled.

Chapter 18

"Shit," Paul Rubenstein muttered. He hunched his collar up against the wind, asking half under his breath, "Why is it cold in St. Petersburg?" He looked around him, down at the Harley between his legs, at the Schmeisser slung under his right arm. He decided nothing in view could or would answer him. He stared down at the road, watching the troops moving along it. "Cubans," he muttered to himself.

Pushing his wire-framed glasses up from the bridge of his nose, Rubenstein let out the Harley's stand, dismounted, and moved into the trees to get further off the road below and to avoid the wind. He dropped to the ground, squatting there. He wished he'd started smoking again.

He could still see the road through the trees, and he watched to make certain none of the troops moving along below him made any sudden moves toward the side of the road, indicating they'd somehow detected his presence. He wished he spoke Spanish. Then perhaps if he got closer to them he could learn something.

"Everybody can't be John Rourke," he said half-aloud, smiling. He wondered for an instant what Rourke was doing. Had he found Sarah and the children yet? If he hadn't, how long would he keep on looking?

Rubenstein studied the road, drawing casually in the dirt between his legs with the point of the Gerber MkII knife Rourke had given him for the journey. He began mentally to tick off the situation's pertinent details, to help himself to form a plan. He had been in the St. Petersburg area for nearly three days. The city itself was partially destroyed; there were internment—concentration—camps all over. He studied the faces inside, behind the wire fences. He'd convinced himself most of the people inside were old and that most of them seemed to be Jewish like himself. It was just a feeling, he knew. Maybe they weren't Jewish; perhaps it was the armed guards and the barbed wire that made him think so—and he had seen films of the camps during World War II. That was enough. He decided some of them were Jewish at least.

He had left his bike and slipped quietly through the streets at night past the Communist Cuban patrols. The house his parents had lived in was gone. There was a house if a roof and three standing walls counted, but there had been a fire and obvious looting. They were not there. He had checked throughout the neighborhood, trying to remember which houses had belonged to friends of his parents from the few times he had visited them there. He hadn't been certain of any of it, but none of the houses in the neighborhood looked to be inhabited anymore, nor habitable.

"Gotta," he muttered, staring away from the road, looking at the meaningless lines he'd drawn in the dirt with the long-bladed knife. There was one large camp, larger than many of the others combined. Somewhere inside, he told himself, there would be someone who knew his parents, perhaps knew what had happened to them. If they were dead, he wanted to know. For certain.

Concentration camps, he told himself, were made to keep people in, not out. The young man smiled. Perhaps after he penetrated the main camp and learned what he could, he could free some of the prisoners. Rourke would, he decided.

Chapter 19

Rourke rolled the Harley Davidson to a stop in the sand. He could appreciate more realistically how thinly spread the Russians must have been. The beach area had been fenced with barbed wire—he'd cut that. But there were no guards in sight. "Stupid," he muttered.

"What did you say?" Sissy asked, sitting behind him on the bike, her grip around his midsection relaxed now that they had stopped.

"I said the Russians are stupid to leave the coast unguarded like this—good thing for us, though." Rourke decided, and without much of a valid reason, he didn't like the girl.

"Oh," she said, noncommittally, almost inaudibly.

"Oh," he echoed, staring down at the surf. He could see a light, blinking from offshore in the twilight. Rourke reached into the belt under his jacket where he'd temporarily stashed the Kel-Lite. He glanced up and down the beach. Then Rourke moved the switch one position forward, pushing the button, releasing it, then pushing it again. He made a series of dots and dashes and, after a moment, the light from offshore, already seeming closer, signaled back in a predetermined pattern he'd worked out with Reed by radio. He moved the switch on the flashlight back into the off position, then handed Sissy the light. "Put that in the side pocket over there."

"Where?"

"In the pack, Sissy—in the pack."

"All right," she said. "Was that the airplane?"

"The amphibious plane, right."

"Are you going to leave your motorcycle behind?" she asked, her voice sounding strained to him. Watching the approaching plane across the water, he decided she was probably wrestling with getting the Kel-Lite back into the Lowe pack.

"No, I'm bringing the bike. They can get close enough I can get it up a ramp and into the plane. Shouldn't get the bike too wet. I can clean off the salt water as soon as we're airborne."

"Can't you just get another motorcycle?" she asked.

"Why should I? There's nothing wrong with this."

"But isn't it a lot of bother—I mean, cleaning it off, hauling it aboard? Why not just—"

"Did you like disposable things—when there were disposable things? Pens, cigarette lighters, things like that?"

"Yes, I suppose I did," she answered, her tone defensive Rourke thought.

"Good for you. I didn't." Rourke said nothing else. Already, the amphibious, twin-engine aircraft was closing on the surf. He gunned the Harley down the sandy embankment to meet it.

Chapter 20

"Miami Beach was the home of so many capitalists—it is appropriate that I have taken the finest home along the beach and made it headquarters for the People's Army."

Natalia smiled, studying Diego Santiago's fleshy, slightly sweating face. She remembered the file. Diego was correct, but Santiago was an assumed last name, ever since his rise to prominence in the Cuban Communist hierarchy.

"General Santiago?" she asked.

"Si, Major Tiemerovna," he responded.

She smiled at him again, then looked out over the veranda and across the sand toward the inky blackness ridged with white foam, the breakers. "All of this—doesn't it distract you? It would me, I confess," she said and laughed a little.

"*You* would distract me, Senorita. I use this house because it is centrally located; it fills my needs. I swim.

97

It is the only exercise my demanding schedule allows me. Perhaps, while you and Colonel Miklov are here with us, you too can go for a swim. It is relaxing. I find it so at least." He smiled again, then, looking at her glass, asked, "More wine?"

She smiled. "A little, I suppose—but only a little, Comrade General."

"You are too formal, Senorita. There is no need for a beautiful woman ever to be formal. Call me Diego. I insist. Take it as an order, if you like, from a superior officer in an allied army."

She smiled, taking his outstretched right hand, feeling it to be slightly clammy. She watched his eyes watching her cleavage.

She leaned back in her chair, her hand slipping from Diego Santiago's hand, then resting on the white table-cloth. She studied the hand, knowing, feeling Santiago's eyes studying her. She had arrived with Miklov, expecting nothing to do with Santiago until morning, feeling emotionally drained after her uncle's revelation. She had felt tired, confused when Santiago's aide met them at the airport, announcing there was a formal late supper being served in two hours. She glanced to her Rolex watch. It was nearly eleven.

With Miklov, the aide had had them driven to Santiago's house along the beach—another surprise. She had brought formal attire—she always did on an assignment such as this. While Miklov had changed, she had showered, washed her hair, dried it, then dressed. Looking at herself in the full length mirror before coming down to dinner she had done two things—slipped an ultra light, thin boot knife into a garter holster on the inside of her left thigh, then checked her appearance. She wore a black evening gown, not too much jewelry, black shoes and a small black bag—her COP derringer pistol was in the bag. She didn't worry that it would be discovered. If Santiago had reason to suspect her as KGB, he'd suspect her all the more without a weapon. And an obvious weapon was always a good thing—it sometimes ended a search quickly enough that a hidden weapon, like the knife on her thigh, would not be found.

Now she moved uncomfortably in the chair, straightening her skirt, moving her eyes from her hand to her shoes, then up her ankle to the hem of her dress. Santiago was talking to Miklov and she was trying to appear disinterested.

"I think, Colonel Miklov, that there is no cause for alarm for your superiors. It is only natural to assume that two dynamic nations such as ours operating in such close proximity as we do should, from time to time, become abrasive with one another. Yet it is this very dynamism and this very strength which makes us allies. How is the expression in English—the fortunes of war, no?"

Natalia looked up from the hem of her dress, seeing Diego Santiago's eyes watching her. "But, Comrade General—Diego," she asked, her voice low, soft—and she intended it to sound that way. "If we are both such worthy allies, then why cannot we learn to function like well-oiled cogs in the Communist machine—together?" She looked into the Cuban's eyes, smiling.

"My dear young woman—you are exquisitely beautiful and you are also very intelligent. You have brought us exactly back to square one, have you not.

Senorita, I am overwhelmed," and Santiago bowed toward her.

The skin on her shoulders, her throat—all the parts of her that were naked to Santiago's eyes—crawled under his gaze, but she leaned forward, knowing he could look down her dress more easily. "Comrade General," she almost whispered. "I do not understand. This beautiful house, this dinner—I was very fatigued when we arrived."

"Perhaps then a swim, as I suggested." Then Santiago, as if he had forgotten Miklov existed, suddenly remembered he did. "You are welcome to join us, Colonel."

Miklov, gray, with tight jowls and dark eyes, smiled. "The young lady is correct. I too am tired, and I'm afraid age precludes a midnight swim. I should be in bed. It has been a long day and I eagerly anticipate our renewed discussions tomorrow."

"Comrade Colonel," Santiago said, "tomorrow, I shall show you both the cream of the armed forces of the People's Democratic Republic of Cuba." Then, turning to Natalia, Santiago said, "But tonight, Senorita, I will show you the ocean. In my humble role as leader of the People's Army, as I have indicated to you, the water is my one form of solace, of rest, of renewal. Perhaps, since these waters touch my home-land of Cuba—perhaps I feel from them the renewal to go on, despite all obstacles. They touch my home, my heart. You can understand this, Senorita?"

"Yes," Natalia answered, watching his eyes.

"You will join me then for a swim?"

"Si," she answered, smiling, watching his eyes smiling. "That is the right word, yes?"

"Very right, Senorita," Santiago answered.

"Gentlemen," she began, standing. Both Miklov and Santiago stood then as well. "Comrade General, I shall meet you—"

"On the beach in fifteen minutes—just beyond the veranda. That gives you sufficient time?"

"Yes," she smiled. Miklov moved her chair back as she walked past the table, saying to her, "Good night, Comrade Major."

She turned, her eyes focused on his. "Yes, Comrade Colonel." And then, as she passed Santiago, his hand was out, as if to help her. She touched her left hand to it and dipped her eyes slightly. He was shorter than she was, and she didn't wish him to become too aware of it.

"I shall be with you, then," she said, softly, noncommittally. It was a game she had played before, and sincerely wished she would not have to play to the ending.

She walked away from the table, through the dining room and to the double oak doors. She stopped, turning around, noticing Santiago's eyes on her—and Miklov's as well. She did nothing, standing there a moment, as if hesitant, then turned and walked through the open door and toward the circular staircase. Santiago could perhaps still see her, she thought. She stopped at the base of the stairs, her left hand catching up the ankle-length skirt of her black dress just above the knee, raising it to help her walk the stairs, her right hand touching lightly at the railing of the bannister. She ascended the stairs, hoping Santiago were watching; she wanted him to have a good show.

She looked down behind her a moment, then continued her ascent to the upper landing, dropping her skirt as she walked toward her room.

There was no need for a key, and none had been provided for her. She turned the knob on the door and entered the room. She had determined earlier it was not video-monitored and assumed nothing had been added to it since her absence. She closed the door behind her and leaned hard against it, staring down at the blue carpet beneath her black shoes, sighing, breathing hard. "Pig," she muttered, but so that only she could hear it, in case there were indeed microphones hidden in the room which she had not detected.

Natalia closed the deadbolt from the inside and walked across the room, tossing her black purse with the COP derringer on the bed.

She stopped in front of the full length mirror. "A midnight swim," she muttered.

She stood in front of the mirror. Behind it, she thought, there might be a camera, so she began to undress as if for some unseen audience. She raised her hands to her hair, pulling the pins that bound it up at the nape of her neck, letting it fall, then shaking it to her shoulders and past that. She hunched her shoulders forward, her arms behind her as she fumbled for the zipper at the back of the black dress, getting the hook and eye closure open.

She pulled the zipper all the way past her waist, then hunched her shoulders again as she slipped the strap that had held the dress up around her neck over her head, letting the front of the dress drop forward, dropping the dress to the floor. She wore no bra, and as the dress fell, she moved her hands up, cupping her breasts in them, then shifting her body to let the dress fall around her ankles. She pushed the slit, lace-trimmed black slip down from her waist, past her hips, and down her thighs to around her ankles. She stared at herself in the mirror. She wore black, lace-trimmed bikini panties, and these she pushed down with her thumbs, after removing the knife on the garter. She bent over, her thumbs hooked on each side of the stocking on her right leg.

She pushed the left stocking down to her ankle, then the right, then stepped out of the dress, the slip, and the panties and pulled her left leg up, rolling the dark nylon from her feet. She stood in front of the mirror, as if surveying herself, turning, looking at her legs, cupping her hands under her breasts.

Natalia decided enough was enough. She turned abruptly away from the mirror, then walked into the bathroom. She assumed that if anything were fixed to provide a picture—short of fiber optics, evidence of which she had seen none—it was the mirror. She sat on the toilet, feeling relatively safe.

Finished, she did what she normally would, then stood, walking back into the bedroom, to her suitcase. There were two bathing suits there—both one-piece. She picked the black one rather than the tan, flesh-colored one. She walked back toward the mirror, holding the suit up in front of her. She turned, flashing her rear end toward the mirror, then walked back toward the bed, sitting on its edge. She put the suit on ducking her head under the strap which would support the front of the suit from her neck.

She walked back to the mirror, adjusting the suit, intentionally cupping her hands under her breasts as she fitted the suit to her body. She did a full turn in the mirror, then walked away from it, again feeling enough was enough.

She took a white, hip-length beach jacket from her suitcase—she hadn't had the time to unpack. Slipping it on, she belted it too tightly about her waist. There was a pair of black, high-heeled sandals in the other suitcase; and, barefoot, she walked across the carpet, found the shoes and put them on.

She walked back to the mirror again. She pulled the earrings off, unclasped the necklace, then looked at the gold Rolex on her wrist. Her timing was perfect—five minutes late.

As she started across the room, she stopped, pausing beside the dresser, taking up a bottle of Chanel No. 9. She used it on her neck and behind her left ear, then picked up the black bag she had tossed on the bed. She opened the bag, took the COP pistol and broke it open, checking the four, 125-grain jacketed hollow points there, then closed the pistol. She replaced it in the bag, then clutched the bag to herself as she started toward the doorway. She sighed. It promised to be a long night, she thought.

Chapter 21

Sarah Rourke slipped down from the rough wooden pier and into the icy water. She pushed her dark hair back from her eyes, looking around her, listening for sounds other than the lapping of the water against the pilons supporting the wooden walkway above.

She'd considered carrying the boning knife in her teeth—aside from pirates in movies, she'd seen John do that once, years ago. They'd been swimming with friends, and a child's foot had gotten entangled in something below the surface. John Rourke, seemingly without considering what to do at all, had simply snatched a knife from somewhere, clamped it between his teeth, and jumped overboard, moments later surfacing with the child—saving the little boy's life.

But she decided against carrying the knife in her teeth, reasoning that if she accidentally dropped it, the knife would fall to the bottom and be lost.

She began to swim, having treaded water sufficiently

long enough to get her body accustomed to the cold. She'd swum in high school and kept it up as a sport over the years until she could almost outswim John. As she moved as soundlessly as possible through the water, she thought about that. She could almost do it as well as John, her husband. Was that the problem? She'd once been sitting in her studio at the farm house, John drinking coffee, watching her work. She'd asked him to trade places with her, to sit at her work table and try his hand at a sketch. He'd been reluctant, but she'd insisted and he had finally agreed. He hadn't wanted to draw from imagination, but she'd insisted on that too. After ten minutes she looked—against his protests—at the sketch. It was of two men, fighting in some jungle. The detail of their muscles, limbs, the expressions on their faces, the detail of the foliage around them—all of it had been almost photographically perfect, as far as he'd gone. But he hadn't finished it.

She'd begun to wonder then if there were anything John Rourke couldn't do when he half tried. But she realized Rourke never *half* tried. It was always one hundred per cent with him.

She stopped, treading water again. The boat she wanted to steal was just ahead of her and, except for the distant and shadowy form of a Soviet guard at the far end of the pier, there was no one in sight. She tucked down under the water, swimming toward the boat. The owner had a sense of humor, she thought. The name on the boat was *Ta-ob,* "boat" spelled backwards.

With Michael and little Annie helping, she had gotten Harmon Kleinschmidt out of the farmhouse and on Sam, John's horse. Michael had ridden with him, to alert her if the wounded Resistance fighter began to pass out or fall from the saddle.

There was a farm some ten miles off where Kleinschmidt had friends—a man in his seventies and his wife, the woman perhaps in her late sixties. The man, Arlo Coin, had agreed to keep the horses and agreed to use his pickup truck to get Sarah and the others near Savannah. He had converted the engine to run on pure alcohol, this distilled from weeds and grass on his farm. He had told Sarah he had been doing it for years before the War and saw no problems with keeping it up. Coin had insisted on helping them once they'd hidden the truck, stating flatly that Kleinschmidt was too weak to walk unaided and too heavy for Sarah or the children to handle. Sarah had agreed, but reluctantly. Then Kleinschmidt had told her not to worry. Reaching under his coat he'd pulled a revolver. She remembered, as he showed it to her, Coin saying, "Smith & Wesson .38/44 Heavy Duty—one of the best guns anybody ever made. Had her since 1937. Never needed another."

Sarah stopped now, touching the hull of the *Ta-ob* under the water, then surfacing, taking in air. Despite the swim, she was cold with just the shorts and T-shirt on. She waited in the water, listening for any sign of someone on deck or in the cabin; there were no lights. She swam toward the bow, stopping, finding a small ladder along the starboard side. She reached out, grabbing the first rung, then started up, the boning knife secure in a plastic bag tied at her waist. As she stepped out of the water and stood crouched on the ladder, the air temperature and the night wind chilled her even more.

She ripped the knife from the bag with her left hand; her right grasped to the railing on the side of the ladder.

Then, the knife clenched in her left fist, she peered up over the side and into the boat. Nothing.

Sarah went up the rest of the ladder and swung onto the deck, the knife transferred to her right hand now. Still in a crouch to stay below the level of the sides of the boat, she moved aft, finding the angular, ladder-like steps leading below. The transom was not locked. She assumed that was some Soviet edict, allowing for easier inspection of the boats at the pier. She started down the steps, into the darkness, leaving the transom open a crack above her.

As she reached the below deck cabin, Sarah Rourke froze. Clearly she heard footsteps on the deck just above her head. She shivered, but it wasn't the cold and the wetness of her improvised swimsuit. The transom lid was opening.

Chapter 22

Rourke, his coat off, his pistol belt and rifle on the floor beside him, leaned back in the leather easy chair and looked down into the fireplace.

"Do you always wear those guns in that shoulder holster? I'd think they would feel just so heavy." Sissy remarked.

Rourke didn't look away from the fire. "It feels uncomfortable when you're first getting used to it, but I've been wearing a double holster for a long time. I don't really notice it anymore. It feels more uncomfortable to be unarmed," Rourke added.

He lit a cigar with his Zippo, then stood up, feeling like a caged animal. He wanted Chambers to show up; he wanted Chambers to comprehend the magnitude of the impending Florida disaster; he wanted Chambers to take the ball. Rourke would then get air transport to Florida, attempt to find Paul if there was time, help Paul find his parents, then get out. There were still

Sarah and the children to locate, somewhere in northern or east-central Georgia.

Rourke studied the flickering of the fire's flames. He knew what had to be done, but wondered if Chambers would have the sense to do it. It was the only reason Rourke had decided to take the offered flight to U.S. II headquarters near the Louisiana-Texas border.

There was a highly polished, twelve-inch Bowie knife on a plaque over the mantle. Rourke studied it intently. Double quillon guard of brass, this, too, highly polished. He reached up, feeling the false edge—it was sharp.

"Rourke—is it Doctor Rourke or Mr. Rourke?—I can never decide what I should call you, sir!"

Rourke turned around, noticing that the woman was already standing. Slowly, eyeing Chambers, Rourke said, "Mr. President, it's good to see you again."

"And you must be Sissy Wiznewski, the seismologist who has some alarming news for us," Chambers said, taking a few steps toward the girl. He shook her hand warmly.

Rourke watched, listened—he decided Samuel Chambers was a somewhat different man, perhaps now more used to being President. But President of what, Rourke wondered?

"Tell the President the alarming news, Sissy," Rourke said, echoing Chambers's tone.

"I don't know where to begin."

"I do," Rourke interrupted, resenting the time being wasted. "She belonged to a group of scientists studying fault lines and earthquake activity in the Appalachian chain, part of a comparative survey with the San Andreas fault line on the Continental and Pacific

110

plates. Most of their instruments kept working after the Night of the War. Correct me if I screw up anything," Rourke said to Sissy, then continued to address Chambers. "They began picking up readings on what appears to be a massive artificially created fault line—probably a result of the bombing on the Night of the War. Anytime now, certainly within the next few days, there will be a massive quake, similar to the one along the San Andreas line that caused California to separate from the Continental plate and fall into the sea. The Florida Peninsula will separate from the Florida Panhandle. It's a lead-pipe cinch according to her instruments.

"That cover it?" Rourke concluded.

"More or less."

"Mother of God!" Chambers sank down into the leather easy chair Rourke had vacated moments earlier.

Rourke lit a cigar, snapping the butt of the old one into the fireplace after firing the fresh one with it.

"That just—just can't be," Chambers sighed, his voice a stammering monotone.

"Here, Mr. President." Sissy Wiznewski handed Chambers the one seismograph printout that she'd carried under her coat when Rourke had rescued her from the Brigands. "If you have a science advisor available, he could certainly confirm the readings. He might interpret them differently, but I don't see where there's any choice really."

"What do you mean?" Chambers looked up at her, the lines in his face deepened.

"Well, I mean, I don't want to presume—"

"Evacuate as much of Florida as you can while

there's still time, if there's still time," Rourke interjected.

"Yes, that's it, really—we have to—"

"Wait," Chambers interrupted. "Evacuate? Florida? The Cuban Communists control it, how could we?"

"There's a way, to do *something* at least," Rourke began, stepping away from the mantle, standing in front of Chambers's chair.

"I don't—"

"You don't have the airpower, and even if you did, you need a truce with the Communist Cubans. You probably need their help."

"Their help!"

"I think I know a way we can get it—from the Russians."

"You're crazy, Rourke. They want to see us dead."

"Maybe they do," Rourke told him. "Maybe there's an advantage in this for them, too, though. If we don't get some sort of truce for the duration of this thing— this should be the greatest loss of life in recorded history, with the exception of the Night of the War itself."

Chambers, his eyes glassy and hard-set, stared up at Rourke. "What do we do?"

"Has Captain Reed told you there's a traitor in U.S. II?"

"A traitor? What do you mean?"

"I'll explain, but right now in order to contact General Varakov, I've got to find the traitor—fast." Rourke turned around, faced the hearth a moment. Then he snapped the glowing cigar butt into the fire. The fire was undisturbed. Rourke hoped what he had said to Chambers had greater impact.

Chapter 23

Sarah Rourke clutched the boning knife, drawing back as tightly as possible against the starboard bulkhead at the base of the steps. She could hear the transom lid creaking open above her at the head of the steps. There was a cold rush of air as the transom opened. A beam of light followed—not natural light, she thought, but a flashlight. She watched, hardly daring to breathe, feeling the water dripping down from her hair, her blue T-shirt, her pink shorts.

Her eyes opened wider as the flashlight beam stopped, the light unwavering on a puddle of water on the floor where she had just stood. She heard a voice from the top of the steps, a man's voice; but the words were unintelligible to her—Russian. She didn't move.

The voice came again, but this time in halting English. "Who is ever down here, come out or I shoot you!"

She pressed her wet shoulder blades back harder

against the bulkhead, wishing she'd brought a gun, perhaps wrapped the .45 automatic in plastic or something. "Who is ever here, come out. Now!"

Again, she remained motionless. She heard the voice—in Russian this time—grunt a word. She was happy she didn't know what the word meant. She could hear footsteps starting down the steps, toward her.

Sarah raised the knife, not really thinking about it, but suddenly aware that she was holding it up, ready to drive it down.

The footsteps stopped; she could see a uniformed back, a Russian soldier's cap, the profile of a rifle in the hands. She tried to move the knife downward, but couldn't. The man's back was within inches of her. She held her breath.

She watched, feeling as though she were witnessing a scene unfolding in a movie. He was turning around, now facing her. The light was in her eyes, and in the gray area beyond the light she could barely discern the features of the man belonging to the Russian voice. "Your hands up!"

"No!" She screamed, hammering the knife down out of the shadow beyond the light. The knife drove into the front of the uniformed body, her right wrist feeling as though it would break as the knife stopped.

There was a loud sound of metal falling to the deck between them—the rifle, she realized. There was a hand coming at her, the hand holding the flashlight moving too, the light weaving in a crazy pattern on the cabin ceiling. She felt the hand closing around her throat. She pulled back on the knife handle, almost falling and losing her balance as the knife pulled free from the soldier's chest. She could see the flashlight moving, raising high, then coming down. She moved the knife again, punching it straight forward in her hand.

The flashlight clattered to the deck; Sarah felt something warm and wet all over her right hand. She reached up with her left hand, the soldier's right hand still on her throat. She was starting to black out, trying to pry the fingers loose. Then she started to fall forward, the soldier's body under her in the darkness of the deck. She let go of the knife, fighting to breathe. He was strong.

With both hands she pried at his fingers, the grip loosening a little. She reached behind her, catching up the flashlight, hammering the flashlight against the hand, the fingers falling away from her throat.

The flashlight slipped from her fingers. As she picked it up, she saw red-fingerprints on the lens, like something over an illuminated microscope. Her fingers were sticky with blood.

She started to get up, then stopped. Crouched, leaning against the bulkhead, she spoke: "God . . ." She dropped the flashlight, closing her eyes. Her knife blade had sliced down through the soldier's cheek and imbedded in his throat. Those dead eyes—she could still see them in the darkness, staring at her.

Chapter 24

Natalia found her way beyond the veranda to the beach, looking up and down its length and not seeing Diego Santiago. She smiled. It would have amused her if after she had intentionally solicited the swim he stood her up.

"Diego?" she said, looking at the dark, white-crested surf. "Diego?" There was no answer.

She turned, starting back up the beach, then heard a shout from behind her and turned back to look toward the water. "Here, Natalia, here!"

She raised her right arm for a long, lazy wave toward the figure she saw emerging from the surf, running up the beach toward her. There was enough moonlight that she could see him well. It was Santiago, wet from the swim, his black, curly hair plastered to his forehead. He stopped a yard away from her.

"Turn around so I can look at you," he commanded. She smiled. As she turned a full 360 degrees, she opened the white jacket belted around her waist; the jacket dropped from her shoulders and back to her elbows as she faced him again. "Do you approve, Comrade General?"

"Si—yes, I do indeed, Comrade Major."

Santiago laughed and so did Natalia. He started toward her and she took a step nearer to him. As he reached out his arms, she turned around. "Thank you," she said and shrugged the rest of the way out of the white terry cloth jacket. There was a white-painted metal chair a few feet away by the seawall and she pointed toward it. "Would you?"

"Of course," Santiago said, his voice less filled with enthusiasm. She handed him the bag. He looked at her. "This is very heavy."

"I have my gun in it," she told him, smiling.

"Ha-ha! Honest—I like that." Santiago laughed, then strode across the sand. She watched him as he set the jacket and purse on the chair, then turned to face her.

"I will race you into the water!" she shouted, running across the sand, her shoes kicked away.

Natalia hit the water, hearing the heavy breathing of Santiago beside her. Throwing herself into the surf as the waves flowed around her legs, she then swam out over the first ridge of breakers. The water felt cold to her. She hadn't swum in an ocean for more than a year, she recalled. She turned toward the beach, swimming until she could stand, then walking from the surf, hugging her hands against her elbows, seeing Santiago coming out of the water a few feet away from her.

"Senorita Natalia, por favor . . ."

She turned back and looked at him, brushing hair

back from her forehead. "What is it, Diego?" Natalia said.

He walked toward her and this time she did nothing, standing there, waiting for what she knew was inevitable. "What is it, Diego?" she repeated.

"Are you trying to seduce me, or to make me seduce you?" he asked, water dripping from his mustache and from the dark hair on his chest.

"Don't be silly," she told him.

"Then why are you here with me, now?"

"I like the ocean," she told him honestly. Then, looking into his eyes, she said softly, "I'm cold now."

He took a step closer and she let him put his arms around her, felt his hands on her wet back. She closed her eyes as she felt him kiss her. It was not as easy as it had been before, she thought, when she had only been married but not yet in love.

Chapter 25

Rubenstein muttered, "God!" The thing crawling quickly around the base of the palm tree behind which he was hidden looked to be the largest roach he'd ever seen in his life. *"Eyuck!"* he hissed to himself. He'd read an article once about roaches, and it surprised him not at all that they survived the Night of the War. Some scientists theorized that if all other life on the planet were to be killed, roaches and rats might still thrive. This was a wood roach or American cockroach, he thought.

Smiling, pushing his glasses up off the bridge of his nose, he saluted the creature, muttering, "My fellow American . . ." He stared beyond the palm now where his real fellow Americans were. Some of the faces he had observed for the last few hours were Hispanic-looking, probably anti-Communist Cubans; some of the faces looked Central European in origin; and some, he thought, were Jews, like himself. The barbed wire was the part that nauseated him, with people living behind it.

He had left the motorcycle about a mile back in a wooded area, then come the rest of the way on foot. After scouting the perimeter of the camp, he had selected the spot least visible between the guard towers and decided on it as his point of entry. He had brought the big Gerber knife, the Browning High Power and the Schmeisser and spare loaded magazines for each of the guns.

He smiled, remembering how, just prior to leaving, Rourke had tried to talk him out of the Schmeisser. "What are you going to do for spare parts? What about extra spare magazines? You'd be better off with something else." But, for once not taking Rourke's advice, Rubenstein had decided to keep the gun he called the "Schmeisser"—despite the fact Rourke had told him repeatedly it was an MP-40. He was familiar with it and liked the firepower it afforded.

Rubenstein studied the camp, smiling to himself—a weapon originally developed for the Nazi war machine was now going to help him to break into a concentration camp and perhaps break some of the inmates out.

It was a good hundred yards from the farthest edge of the tree line to the outer fence, Rubenstein estimated. He had searched the St. Petersburg area and found a deserted farm implements store, the windows smashed and yet a few items remaining there. He had scanned the place for radiation with the Geiger counter on his Harley Davidson, then stolen a pair of long-handled wire cutters. Rubenstein remembered when he and Rourke had broken into the back room of the geological supply store and stolen the flashlights that first night they had teamed up. Rourke had explained then that it was no longer stealing, it was foraging.

Rubenstein smiled at the thought: he had foraged wire cutters.

Beyond the first wire fence was a barren patch, extending perhaps twenty-five yards. Rubenstein had studied the ground through the armored Bushnell 8x30s he carried—identical to the ones Rourke used. He could see no signs of recent digging, no signs of depressions in the sparsely grassed ground. He hoped it was not mined.

At the end of the twenty-five yards of open ground was another fence, ten feet high, and this one might be electrified. He wasn't certain; but the way no one of the guards ever walked close to it made him wonder. Beyond that was another ten feet or so of open ground, then a six-foot-high barbed wire fence. Against this fence people were leaning, staring out. At what they stared he didn't know. He wondered if they knew.

It had been dark for several hours; he had observed the pattern of the guards.

He checked the Timex on his left wrist—he'd decided to go exactly on the hour, and that was five more minutes.

Chapter 26

Sarah Rourke wished she had a watch. She looked up, trying to determine the time by the position of the moon, but couldn't. She slowed the boat, then brought it to a stop, realizing for the first time that had she not killed the young Russian guard, he would likely have alerted the harbor patrol and she would never have gotten far from the pier. She walked back to the aft portion of the boat. She had dragged the young man's body up from below deck earlier, covering it with a tarp she had found. That was nearly an hour ago, and now as she drew back the tarp, she imagined the skin to have grayed appreciably. But she realized that if it had, it would have been impossible to tell in the moonlight. She reached down, trying to touch the body where it was clothed, but her left hand brushed against the man's left hand as she tugged at the inert form. She drew her hand back. The body was cold, unnaturally cold, like a turkey already plucked, frozen, and left to thaw—touching him felt like sticking her hand inside a turkey to take out the giblets on Thanksgiving morning.

Sarah leaned over the rail. She knew that Mr. Coin, Kleinschmidt, and her two children were waiting farther down the beach, and she wanted to be rid of the body before the children saw. Michael had killed a man, with the same knife—but she didn't want Michael or Annie to see this. She turned and looked back at the body, then shook her head, imagining that the left hand had moved. She hadn't closed the eyes and she should have. They were open, gaping, like fish eyes.

The fish, she thought. She was feeding him to the fish.

She leaned down, again trying to grasp the body to pull it toward the portside rail, and again touching the dead hand. She turned, quickly, bending over the railing, vomiting into the water. She wiped the back of her hand across her mouth, feeling colder now in the damp shorts and T-shirt than she had felt before.

She bent down to the dead man again, this time grabbing his arms, her hands touching his—but she held them anyway. She pulled the heavy body toward the portside railing, stopping at the bulkhead beneath it, then wrapping her arms around the dead man's chest. As she hauled him up, she could only see the back of his head. She pulled, shoved, twisted, then positioned the body beside the railing.

Sarah had the sudden, horrible thought that if she didn't have the body weighted it would float to the surface. But she couldn't see herself putting the body down, then getting it up and over to the railing again. She stood the dead soldier up beside the rail, then pushed his body forward, and as the head and upper trunk swung out over the water, she could see the man's face.

She screamed as she let go of the body; it tumbled into the darkness of the water.

Sarah Rourke stood there a moment, her body shaking.

"Got to get going," she muttered to herself. She peered over into the dark water and thought she saw him, the eyes staring up at her. Then she turned and ran forward toward the controls, almost slipping on the blood-stained deck.

Chapter 27

Paul Rubenstein glanced at his wristwatch. Running in a low crouch, he started out of the palms and toward the first of the ten-foot wire fences, the Schmeisser slung from his right shoulder, the wirecutters in his left hand. He was slightly winded by the time he'd crossed the distance to the first fence. And as he reached it he dropped into a deeper crouch, glancing quickly from side to side, the wire cutters already moving in his hands. Starting at the bottom of the fence he clipped a single cut, approximately four feet high. Because of the heaviness of the wire, another cut was needed. He cut horizontally across the top of the first cut, then pulled the barbed wire outward, toward him, slipping through in the darkness and pulling the "gate" in the wire closed behind him. He glanced toward the guard towers, then hit the dirt, flattening himself, the Schmeisser out in his right hand. A searchlight beam crossed over the ground less than a foot away from him.

The searchlight moved on, and so did Rubenstein, running across the grassy area, zigzagging just in case there were a minefield, hoping by some miracle he would miss them all by not running in a straight line. He reached the opposite fence line, breathless again. He started to reach his hand toward it, then stopped, his hand recoiling. There was a rat on the ground less than a foot from him, the body half-burned.

"Electrified," he cursed to himself.

Rubenstein glanced from side to side, quickly trying to determine whether to go back or whether there were some other way to cross the fence. "Damn it!" he muttered, then snatched at the big Gerber knife and started digging in the mixed dirt and sand. He couldn't go through the fence, couldn't go over it—so he'd go under it. He glanced up, flattening himself on the ground, sucking in his breath, almost touching the fence with his bare hand. The searchlight moved down the center of the open space between the fences, missing him by inches. As soon as it passed, keeping himself as low to the ground as possible, he began again to dig.

For once he was grateful he wasn't as big or as broad-shouldered as Rourke, he thought. He scooped dirt with his hands, widening the hole under the fence. The searchlight was making another pass and he flattened himself to the ground, as close to the fence as possible, this time noticing the searchlight that scanned, more frequently and more rapidly, the ground between this fence and the interior fence. That, at least, was not electrified. With the hour, all the prisoners in the compound had been herded inside the tents under which they were sheltered, and the compound grounds were empty of life. But earlier he had seen hands, faces—all touching that fence. It was possible, he thought, as he began again to dig, that the smaller fence was electrified after the compound was cleared, but he had to take the chance.

The small trench under the fence seemed wide enough now and, slipping into position, just missing another pass of the searchlight, he started through on his back. His shirt pulled out of his pants, and he felt the dirt against the skin at the small of his back.

He pushed on, then stopped—the front of his shirt was stuck on a barb in the lowest strand of wire. Perhaps there was no power in the lowest strand, he thought; perhaps the material in the shirt just hadn't made the right contact. He didn't know. He sucked his stomach in lest his skin touch the barb. Rubenstein looked from side to side, past the fence and back toward his feet, seeing the searchlight starting again. It would pass over his feet, reveal his presence.

There was a sick feeling inside him, his mind racing to find a way out. He had to gamble, he thought. He touched, gingerly with his shirt-sleeved elbow, at the wire. Nothing happened. Rubenstein reached out with both hands, freeing the shirt front from the barb, then pushed through, under the wire, the searchlight sweeping over the ground as his feet moved into the shadow. He was through!

The young man got to his feet, still in a crouch. He stared back at the wire a moment, then reached into the pockets of his leather jacket. There was nothing he could use, but he had to know. Taking the wirecutters, he reached under the fence's lowest strand, using the cutters like a slave hand in a laboratory, picking up the dead rat and sliding it under the fence toward him. He looked at the charred creature, and his mouth turned down at the corners in disgust. He hated the things. He lifted the rat with the tips of the cutters and tossed the already-dead body against the wire second from the bottom of the fence. Then he drew back, his right arm going up toward his face. The body clung to the wire a moment, smoking, electrical sparks flying. Paul's stomach churned and he felt like throwing up, but instead watched the searchlight as it swept toward him; then he darted across the few feet of ground to the low fence, hiding beside it, gambling it wasn't electrified as he touched the cutters to the lowest strand, then the one above it.

"Thank God," he whispered, letting out a long sigh. As the light passed inches from where he crouched, he began to cut the wire, using the same pattern he had before, cutting up approximately four feet, then across approximately three feet.

Looking over his shoulder, the wire cutters in his left hand now, he folded back the fence section and started through, into the compound.

He folded the fence section back, in a crouch, the pistol grip of the Schmeisser in his right fist, the muzzle moving from side to side as he surveyed the compound. He could see a guard—one only—walking slowly around the grounds, fifty yards from where he was. Rubenstein, still holding the wirecutters, started toward the nearest tent in a low, dead run. He pushed his way inside the tent.

Paul Rubenstein stopped, the smell that assailed his nostrils nauseating him, a buzzing sound in the air as flies swarmed throughout the tent. He looked in the faces of the people under the glow of the single yellow light hanging from a drop cord in the center of the tent, the flies and moths buzzing close to it. The faces were young, old, all of them weary, some of them sleeping, flies crawling across them. There was a child, moaning beside a sleeping woman. He stepped closer to them, and he kicked away the mouse nibbling at the child's leg.

Paul Rubenstein stood there a moment, tears welling up in his eyes, his glasses steaming a little. In that instant, he was thankful for the guns he carried, for the things he'd learned that had kept him from a similar fate. He was grateful to Rourke for teaching him how to survive after the Night of the War.

The phrase, "My fellow Americans . . ." and how he'd thought of it earlier as the roach climbed around the palm tree beyond the fences, came to his mind. Rubenstein stood there, crying, his right fist wrapped tightly on the Schmeisser.

Chapter 28

Sarah Rourke stood at the wheel of the fishing boat, glancing shoreward, trying to see if she could still locate Mr. Coin in the darkness. She couldn't. "It was rough, wasn't it, Mrs. Rourke?" Harmon Kleinschmidt asked her.

She looked down at the young man seated at her feet as she stood before the controls.

Before she answered him, she looked back to the stern—on the tarp that covered the blood from the dead soldier she could see Michael and Annie, already dozing.

She looked down at Kleinschmidt, saying, "My name is Sarah. You don't need to call me Mrs. Rourke—I'm not that much older than you are. Yes, it was rough, I suppose."

"I saw them bloodstains. You had to kill somebody, didn't you?"

"I thought gentlemen didn't ask questions like that."

"I ain't a gentleman that much—and you sure ain't either, Sarah."

She looked away from the waters ahead of her, and down at the young man again. "What do you mean?" she asked, still cold in her wet things despite the blanket wrapped around her now.

"I'll just come right out with it. What you told me, I don't think it's fair to you or them kids to go on doin' what you're doin'. You need a man to take care of all of you. I guess I'm sort of volunteerin'. I like you—a lot—Sarah."

Her cheeks felt hot. She didn't know what to say to the man—the boy, she thought. He wasn't more than twenty-five, if that.

"That's sweet of you, Harmon."

"Ain't sweet of me, Sarah. I mean what I say."

"A lot of men feel that way about somebody who's helped them, like a nurse for example."

"It ain't that," he told her flatly.

"Well, you just rest," she began.

"I'm sick of restin'—sick of this whole War, the whole damned thing."

"So am I," she said, honestly. "I killed a man with a knife just a little bit ago. My boy, Michael, killed a man. I've killed other people since the Night of the War. We've been cold, sick, wet, dirty; we've gone without sleep. All of it."

"I hear that northeastern Canada didn't get hit much. Fella I met had come down from there, missed the Commies all the way. New York City he heard was all gone, but up in northeastern Canada it was still like before. Ain't nothin' there the Communists would want, I guess—too cold. But a man could have a good

131

life up there, with the right woman, with kids like them."

Sarah looked down at him and wished he weren't sitting so close to her feet. "How far is the island?"

"You still on the compass heading I worked out?"

"Uh-huh."

"Maybe twenty minutes or so. Just keep them runnin' lights out so the patrol boats don't spot us. I figure we could take this boat and make it pretty far up into Canada—leave all this behind us."

"What about the Resistance, the men in prison you told me about?" Sarah said softly.

"I don't know . . . don't guess I'll help them any by gettin' myself killed. I did my share. Sounds like you've done your share too since the War began."

"My husband is out there somewhere, looking for us."

"You don't know that. He might be dead. If he is alive, might figure you and the kids were dead—maybe took up with another woman."

"Maybe," Sarah answered. "Maybe all of that. But if he's alive, he's looking for me. And the only thing that's kept me going is telling myself he's alive."

"What if I tell you he's dead probably; or what if I tell you he's so busy stayin' alive himself that he can't look for you? What if—"

"What if the War had never happened?" She looked back across the bow, searching the shadowy, moonlit horizon for some sign of the offshore island.

"How come he was away from you when it happened? None of my business, I know that. But how come?"

"We—" she began. "We'd been separated. Nothing

132

formal. Just couldn't get along the last few years. He came back, just before the War. We made up, decided to try again. It was my fault, really. He wanted to cancel the job he had in Canada and stay home. I told him I needed the time to get my head clear, to think, so we could start again. The night the War happened he should have been on his way back."

"Driving?"

"No, by air."

"Ain't nothin' left of Atlanta, Sarah, if he landed there. I heard lots of commercial airliners crashed when they ran out of fuel with nowhere to land, or just got blown out of the sky when they flew too close to a missile or an air burst. He's dead—got to be."

"You don't know my husband," she told Kleinschmidt. "He isn't like anybody you ever met."

"He's some kind of super guy or somethin'?"

"In a way, I guess he is. You can see it in Michael. I wouldn't have expected a boy three times Michael's age to do what he's done. It's not normal."

"What do you mean?" Kleinschmidt asked.

A cloud passed in front of the moon. She could no longer see Kleinschmidt's young, tired face when she looked down by her feet where he sat, propped against the bulkhead. "John Rourke is—he's always been so much larger than life. He's almost perfect, really. He seems to know everything, to be able to do anything, to solve any problem. He isn't like you," she told Kleinschmidt. Then, under her breath, so no one but herself would hear, she added, "Or me."

Chapter 29

Rubenstein moved from tent to tent, after having thrown up once he'd gotten outside the first tent, more careful to avoid silhouetting himself against the light. He talked to an older man who'd been awake, swatting flies away from a festering wound on his left leg. The lights were kept on in the tents to make certain no one stood up during the night and to make visual inspection of the tents easier when the guards looked in. There were no sanitary facilities, no facilities for child care, and some of the guards, the old man had confessed, enjoyed beating people. Some of the other guards had seemed like decent men, the old man had told him, but they did nothing when the other guards began their beatings.

The old man had never heard of retired Air Force Colonel David Rubenstein or his wife.

Paul stopped now outside a tent, the fifth so far. Shaking his head, he forced his way inside, keeping low to avoid profiling himself in the yellow light. The stench in this tent was either not so bad, or he had become accustomed to it—he wasn't sure which. There were more children here, faces drawn, eyes sunken, bellies swollen. The old man—Rubenstein hadn't asked his name and the man hadn't volunteered it— had said most of the older people gave the bulk of their food to the children and the recent mothers; and the food allotment for each adult per day was a cup of cereal, as much bad water as you wanted to drink, and twice a week fish or meat. The cereal had weevils in it, the fish and meat usually smelled rancid. A lot of the people around the camp had dysentery, the old man had said.

Rubenstein passed through the tent, looking for his parents, looking for a familiar face, not sure if he'd recognize any of his parents' friends. There was a woman at the far end of the tent, holding a child in her arms, the child's breathing labored. She was awake and as he passed her, she whispered, "Who are you?"

"My name is Paul Rubenstein," he told her, glancing around the tent.

"Why are you here?"

"I'm looking for my parents. Do you know them? My father has a full head of white hair, his first name is David. My mother's first name is Rebecca. Rubenstein. He was a Colonel in the Air Force before he retired."

"He wouldn't be here, then," the woman said.

Rubenstein sucked in his breath, wondering what the woman meant, afraid to ask.

"He just wouldn't be here. I was supposed to be someplace else too," she said, brushing a fly away from her child's lips. "But I was pregnant and they didn't want me along, so they left me. I lost the baby," she said, her voice even. "I don't know what they did with my baby afterward. They never told me about him—he was a boy. My husband Ralph would have been proud of the boy—handsome. Ralph, he's in the Air Force too, that's why they took him. Some kind of special camp near Miami for military people and their families. I hope they don't hurt Ralph. I would have named my baby Ralph Jr., after my husband. He was a beautiful boy. I don't know what they did with him. I would have named him Ralph, you know."

Rubenstein looked at her, whispered, "I'm sorry," then left the tent. He crouched outside by the flap, crying quietly. "Goddamn them," he muttered.

It was starting to rain and in the distance below the dark rain clouds he could see a tiny knife edge of sunlight, reddish tinged. The camp would soon be awake and he had to get out before he got caught. He looked back toward the tent. He could hear the woman talking to herself.

He decided something, then. He was going to go to Miami, find his parents at whatever hellhole camp they were in, if they were still alive. But first he was going to do something here. He didn't know what yet. There was the Army Intelligence contact. Maybe he could help, Rubenstein thought.

Paul pulled himself back against the tent. He heard something, the rumble of an engine. He looked to his right—there was a U.S. military jeep coming, three Cubans riding in it. The rain was coming down in sheets now, and the wind was picking up. Rubenstein pushed his glasses back from the bridge of his nose, brushed his thinning black hair back from his high forehead.

He pulled back the bolt on the Schmeisser, giving it a

solid pat.

Paul Rubenstein raised himself to his feet, standing almost directly in front of the jeep, the headlights beaming just to his left. At the top of his lungs, the young man shouted, "Eat lead, you bastards!" and he squeezed the trigger of the Schmeisser.

"Trigger control," he shouted, reiterating Rourke's constant warning to him, working the trigger out and in, keeping to three-round bursts from the thirty-round magazine. The driver of the jeep slumped forward across the wheel, then the man beside him, the third man in the back raising a pistol to fire. Rubenstein pumped the Schmeisser's trigger again, emptying three rounds into the man's chest. The man fell back, rolling down into the mud.

Rubenstein ran beside the jeep, the vehicle going off at a crazy angle into one of the tents.

The young man jumped for it, his left foot on the running board, his right hand loosing the Schmeisser, pushing the dead driver from behind the wheel. Sliding in, he kicked the dead man's feet away from the pedals.

Rubenstein ground the vehicle to a halt, noticing now for the first time that there was a gray light diffused over the camp. It was dawn. He rolled the body of the passenger, then the driver, out of the right side of the jeep, shifting the vehicle into reverse. People streamed from their tents. As he skidded the jeep around, slamming on the brakes as he fumbled the transmission into first, he could see guards running toward him from the far end of the camp.

His jaw was set, his lips curled back from his teeth, as he stomped on the gas pedal, driving forward. The puddles sloshed up on him as he raced through the mud. Some of the prisoners of the camp threw

137

themselves toward the advancing Cuban guards.

"No!" Rubenstein shouted, the guards machine-gunning the women, the old people.

Rubenstein buttoned out the magazine on the Schmeisser with his left hand, replacing it with a fresh one, the windshield of the jeep down in front of him. He rested the blue-black submachine gun along the dashboard and started firing again.

There were dozens of guards, he thought, all of them armed with assault rifles or pistols, streaming from metal huts. They were half-dressed, shouting, firing at him. Rubenstein kept shooting. He glanced to his left—there was a Communist Cuban guard running beside the jeep, hands outstretched, reaching for him.

Rubenstein balanced the steering wheel with his left knee, snatching the wire cutters from his belt, ramming the eighteen inches of steel behind him and out, then looked back. The Cuban soldier fell, the wirecutters imbedded in his chest.

A smile crossed Rubenstein's lips as he stomped the clutch and upshifted, the jeep now speeding past the tents, the huts, the angry, shouting guards and their guns.

Rubenstein triggered another burst from the Schmeisser, getting a man who looked like an officer. The young man hoped he was the camp commandant.

The Schmeisser was shot dry and he dropped it beside him on the front seat, snatching the worn blue Browning High Power into his right fist, thumbing back the hammer, firing the first round into the face of a Cuban soldier who'd thrown himself up on the hood of the jeep.

The soldier fell away; there was a scream as the jeep rolled over something. Rubenstein didn't care what it was.

The High Power blazing in his right hand, he fought the wheel of the jeep with his left, bringing the vehicle into a sharp left turn, the jeep almost flipping over on him as he gunned it forward. Holding the pistol awkwardly, he rammed the stick into third gear, the engine noise so loud he could barely hear the shouts now.

Two Cuban soldiers were running for him, the gate a hundred yards ahead. Rubenstein rammed the Browning straight out in his right hand, firing once, then once again, the nearer of the two men throwing his hands to his face as he fell. The second man, unhit, dove into the jeep, his hands reaching out for Rubenstein's throat. Rubenstein tried bringing the gun up to fire, but the man was in the way, his hands tightening on Rubenstein's throat as the jeep swerved out of control.

Rubenstein dropped the Browning, clawing at the Cuban's face, getting his fingers into the man's mouth by the left cheek, then ripping as hard as he could.

The man's face split on the left side, the fingers released from Rubenstein's throat, and Rubenstein grasped the 9mm pistol. He snapped back the trigger, the muzzle flush against the Communist soldier's chest, the scream from the torn face ringing loud in Rubenstein's ears as the man fell back, into the mud.

Rubenstein cut the wheel right just in time, the left fender crashing into a row of packing crates that tumbled into the mud. The High Power clenched in his right fist, Rubenstein cut the wheel harder right, with less than fifty yards to go until he reached the main gate. A dozen guards stood by the gate shooting at him.

Paul jammed the Browning High Power into his trouser band, then fumbled on the seat for the

Schmeisser. He buttoned out the empty magazine, balancing the steering wheel with his left knee again as he changed sticks in the submachine gun. He smacked back the bolt, bringing the muzzle of the weapon up over the hood, his left fist locked on the wheel again. He didn't shoot.

The distance to the gate was now twenty-five yards. He hoped he remembered what Rourke had told him about practical firing range. Twenty yards, the guards at the gate still firing. Fifteen yards and Rubenstein began pumping the trigger, two-round bursts this time, firing at the greatest concentration of the guards. One man went down, then another. The guards ran as the jeep rammed toward them.

Rubenstein kept up a steady stream of two-round bursts, nailing another guard. He punched his foot all the way down on the gas pedal as the jeep homed toward the gate, shouting to himself, "Now!" The front end of the vehicle crashed against the wood and barbed wire gate, shattering it. The jeep stuttered a moment, then pushed ahead. Rubenstein brought the SMG back up, firing it out as he cut the wheel into a sharp right onto the road.

As he sped past the concentration camp, the noise of gunfire from behind him had all but stopped. He looked to his right, toward the camp. He could see men, women, and children; he imagined he saw the old man with the festering leg wound who had told him so much, the young woman with the dead baby. Rubenstein began to cry, telling himself it was the wind of the slipstream around the vehicle doing it to his eyes.

Every person in the camp compound was waving his arms in the air, cheering.

Chapter 30

Natalia stood under the water of the shower, the water hot against her body. She'd wanted to wash away more than the sand, she realized. She turned off the water after running it cold for a moment, then stepped out. She grabbed a towel and wrapped it around her hair, then another towel and wrapped it around her body. Her feet still slightly wet as she walked out of the bathroom, across the carpeted bedroom and to the double glass doors at the far end. There she stepped out onto the small balcony overlooking the sea. She was disappointed. She had missed the sunrise.

It was cold, but she stood there a moment, then walked back inside, toweling herself dry and pulling on an ankle-length white robe. She took a cigarette from the dresser and lit it, inhaling deeply. Then, the towel still wrapped around her hair, she walked back out on the balcony, standing by the railing, staring at the beach and the ocean beyond.

It had been a night she wanted quickly to forget. She understood why Diego Santiago was the way he was with a woman. She didn't think it was that she had so excited him. It was a problem that only a man could have, she thought. He had apologized, then fallen silent. She had rubbed his body, kissed him, tried to soothe him afterward. And she felt now that he trusted her, feeling somehow she knew a guilty secret.

She had washed her thighs three times, but the memory of what had happened to Santiago before he'd been able to do what he'd wanted to her still lingered. She would have felt sorry for him normally, she thought. But he was such a lie, such a fake, she thought. The "macho" general was like a young boy.

She was glad nothing had happened with him—because she hadn't wanted it. In the days with Karamatsov she had sometimes used her body to gain information. But she had never liked it, even though Vladmir had told her he would not blame her for whatever she did.

When Santiago kissed her, she had thought only of Rourke, wished it were Rourke, and afterward known that with Rourke it would have been so much different. She hugged her arms about her against the chill of the wind, looking skyward, thinking it was perhaps going to rain.

"John," she whispered.

Rourke had killed Karamatsov, but *for her,* as her uncle had explained it. Should she keep the vow she'd made and kill Rourke?

The uncertainty inside was destroying her, Natalia thought. But more than ever now, she knew, she loved the American. She wondered, absently, if he had yet found his wife and children. Somehow it would be easier to know he was with them. Then he would have no reason to think of her and she would know for herself that he was out of reach.

Natalia smiled, thinking of Rourke, knowing that if she were to fight something that lived only in Rourke's heart she could never win.

Chapter 31

John Rourke downed half the tumbler of whiskey,
looked at his watch, then walked from the table and to
the curtained window. He drew back the curtain,
squinting against the sunlight. There were dark clouds
on the horizon, but above them the sun was bright. He
threw the curtains open, and light filled the room.

He walked across it again, snapping off the lamp
which had illuminated the table through the night and
early morning. He looked at Chambers, then at Sissy
Wiznewski.

"I don't know which one of them is the Communist
agent. The information in their files is too ambiguous."

"It's all we have," Chambers said, his voice sounding old.

"I know that." Rourke nodded. "I trust Reed. I don't
think he's the traitor. Couldn't be just a small fish—
gotta be somebody with access to practically everything you do."

"Why haven't they attacked here?" the girl asked.

Chambers shrugged his shoulders. Rourke answered for him: "To mount a full scale attack here would be time-consuming, expensive, and use a lot of troops the Russians can't spare. As long as they have President Chambers under a microscope, know his every move, it doesn't bother them. It's almost better than capturing him. If they captured him, somebody else would assume the leadership function and they'd be in the dark as to what U.S. II is planning or doing. This way, they know everything. Once we find the traitor, it'll be a different story. I think this area will be too hot for you." He turned to Chambers. "You'll have to leave here, go into hiding somewhere else." He turned and looked back at the girl. "This traitor, whoever he is, is the reason they've left this place alone. In a pinch, they could probably have used the spy they have to assassinate the President anyway. Got the best of both worlds. The KGB people aren't fools enough to cut off their nose to spite their face."

"You're sure there's a traitor here?" Chambers groaned.

"Has to be. There's only one way I can see to flush him out, too. The best ruse is no ruse at all. I want you to call an emergency meeting."

"Why didn't you ever run for President, Mr. Rourke? I'd have voted for you," Chambers smiled.

Rourke smiled back. "Better things to do," he said.

Chapter 32

Sarah Rourke stood on the beach, the blanket over her shoulders, her body still cold. Harmon Kleinschmidt's arm also was around her shoulders—to support himself as he stood, she told herself. Michael and Annie were standing a few feet in front of her. She glanced over her shoulder, at the fishing boat beached in the surf.

She turned back to look up the beach toward the rocks beyond. She'd been following the movement there for some time and now, finally, the people who had been watching her were coming down.

Unarmed, Sarah took a step forward, Kleinschmidt moving beside her.

"Here they come, Sarah," he told her.

She only nodded, watching. About two dozen women were walking across the beach, some of them holding pistols, some with rifles. One woman had a baby suckling her left breast and she held a pistol in her right hand. There were children, too, about Michael and Annie's ages. And most of the women looked young.

Michael looked at her and Sarah nodded, saying, "It's all right, Michael. Here are children for you and Annie to play with. You'll see." She saw him staring at Kleinschmidt, the dark eyes boring toward the man holding her, the jaw set like John's was so often.

"See, Sarah—children for your kids to play with while we wait here."

"Wait?"

"I want you to come with me, Sarah. I mean that. I'll convince you I'm right."

"Hey, Harmon!" A woman holding a baby in one hand and a pistol in the other shouted at him. She stopped, her bare toes moving in the sand as she stood.

"Hey, Mary Beth—this here's Sarah, the children are Michael and Annie—good kids, too."

Sarah watched Michael looking at Kleinschmidt, not liking what she saw in his eyes.

"I'll get somebody to take the boat out and scuttle her," Mary Beth said.

"No you don't," Sarah told her. "I'm just a taxi service. Harmon was wounded, I brought him here. I hope nobody minds if I stay for a little while, let my children rest a little. But then I'm leaving."

"We're both leaving," Harmon entered.

Sarah looked up at him, watching his eyes. She didn't know if she liked what she saw there.

"Then you get it down into the shallows along the beach there." Mary Beth pointed to the left with her pistol. "And get her moored and camouflage it. Them Russians see a boat here, they're gonna come lookin' for us for sure."

"Agreed," Sarah shouted back.

"Come on then," Mary Beth said, smiling for the first time. "I'll give you a hand and watch the kids. Some of the girls here can help you with Harmon, gettin' him up to the cave. Then I guess we can all give you a hand with the boat. Come on." She started toward Michael and Annie, Michael's arm going around his sister's shoulders, his feet moving back across the sand. Mary Beth looked at Michael and Annie. "Suit yourself, boy. Just follow everybody else then."

"See," Harmon Kleinschmidt whispered. "It's gonna be fine."

Sarah just looked at him. He was the only fully grown man on the island and couldn't take more than two steps without someone holding him up. She shook her head, shivering a little, not thinking it was going to be fine at all.

Chapter 33

John Rourke waited in the shadows by the corner of the building, watching. Chambers had called the emergency meeting, not announcing Rourke's arrival but did reveal the presence of Sissy Wiznewski. Chambers had announced to his advisers that disaster in Florida was imminent; he told them everything that had nothing to do with Rourke's plan to flush the traitor. Prior to the meeting, Chambers had selected eleven men, Rourke making the twelfth. The eleven had been chosen from Army Intelligence, men Chambers knew Reed personally trusted.

The meeting finally broke up. Rourke waited. On mere chance, he had selected to follow Randan Soames, commander of the Texas Volunteer Militia. Each of the other men would also follow one of the advisers. If someone left the compound, it would be almost a dead giveaway that this person were the traitor, Rourke had determined.

As he studied the compound, looking for some sign of Soames, Rourke wished it were merely as simple as finding the traitor. But once the traitor was recognized, it would be necessary to follow him to his contact, his radio, whatever means he used to notify the Soviets. And through that chain Rourke could contact Varakov. Already time was running out and there was little hope of an evacuation, however limited.

Rourke turned up the collar of his coat, the wind cold on his neck. He'd left the pistol belt with the Python and the CAR-15 with his bike. As he closed the leather jacket he checked the twin Detonics .45s in the double Alessi rig under the coat—they were secure, with spare magazines for the pistols on his trouser belt in friction retention speed pouches.

Cold still, Rourke hunkered back into the niche in the wall beside which he stood, then stopped. Randan Soames, dressed in a pair of Levis, a black Stetson and a western-style plaid shirt, was walking across the compound toward the gates. It was almost too easy, Rourke thought. As soon as Soames disappeared through the gates, Rourke took off at a dead run after him, reaching the gates, nodding to the guard there and looking down the road. Soames was walking. Rourke turned to the guard. Both the Intelligence people and the MPs were under Reed. "Did he say where he was going, Corporal?"

"No, sir—just for a walk, I guess. He does that a lot, but so do some of the others."

"How long is he usually gone?"

"You're Mr. Rourke, aren't you?"

"That's right, son," Rourke told him.

"Maybe half an hour. But if he were going anyplace on foot, the only place he could make in that amount of

150

time and get back would be the town. It's abandoned now, and there wouldn't be time for him to do anything except turn around and walk right back."

"He always walks that way?" Rourke said, pointing down the road.

"Leastways every time I've seen him, sir."

"Thanks, Corporal." Rourke smiled, starting down the road after Soames, hugging the compound wall until the man disappeared over the rise. Then he started running as fast as he could, getting to the rise and dropping down beside the road.

Randan Soames wasn't walking quickly, wasn't turning around—nothing suspicious. Rourke waited. Maybe all Soames was doing was going for a walk—for a man his age he looked reasonably fit, and riding a desk all day could make any man antsy. He watched Soames pass over the next rise—there wasn't even a weapon visible. Rourke couldn't see anyone going out these days unarmed unless he were a complete fool.

Rourke ran ahead to the next rise, barely catching sight of Soames as he finally looked behind him, then pushed his way into a stand of trees. Rourke watched, waiting, thinking that a radio might be concealed in the trees there. But as Rourke started to push himself up, to move over the rise toward the trees, Soames reappeared, pushing a small motorcycle. A smile crossed Rourke's lips, then the corners of his mouth turned down. It was a small Honda, the kind that had been made years earlier and designed for compactness—the handlebars folded down for easy storage. He remembered reading about the small cycle. Top speed was about thirty-five miles per hour he recalled.

Soames looked from side to side along the road, then mounted the cycle, starting it and continuing down the road toward the abandoned town.

Rourke realized now how Soames made his walk so quickly and made it appear he had no time to do anything if he did walk down to the town. It had to be risky keeping the cycle stowed there, Rourke thought. But being a spy was not exactly safe either, he knew.

There was nothing to do now but run. Rourke pushed himself to his feet and took off along the rise, wishing he'd somehow had the foresight to stash his own motorcycle nearby, or that he could risk a radio call-in and get transportation. But he had no idea what frequency Soames's Soviet contact might be on, and had eschewed the use of a radio. So he ran, stripping the leather jacket from his back and holding it bunched in his left fist.

He had to gamble that Soames would be headed for the town and stay on or near the road. The small bike Soames rode wouldn't handle the terrain off the road— or at least Rourke hoped it wouldn't. The road, he remembered from the map he had studied earlier, zig-zagged following the terrain, and Rourke ran cross-country now to intercept the road.

He skidded down a low embankment, rolling behind some scrub brush, low against the ground, the road below him as Soames moved along it on the small bike. As Soames passed, Rourke pushed himself up, running across the road and through the grassy field beyond, to intercept the road again just before it turned into the town. His face and neck streaming sweat, his arms back and out like a distance runner going for the tape, Rourke ran on, not daring to lose sight of Randan Soames.

Rourke stopped again, diving half into a ditch along the roadside as Soames rounded a curve.

The commander of the Texas paramilitary forces stopped the bike, looking behind him, then from side to side. Rourke, peering through the tall grass, could see a smile crossing Soames's face. The bike started up again, down the road and into the town.

Rourke pushed himself up, jumping the ditch into the road, then crossing it and running parallel to it, hoping he was in the rider's blind spot should Soames look back. Rourke reached the building at the nearest edge of the abandoned town.

The town-limits sign was down, but he estimated from the buildings and the streets, that it had been a town of three or four thousand before the Night of the War.

He peered around the corner of the abandoned fire station behind which he stood, watching as Soames turned the motorcycle down the street at the farthest edge of the town.

Rourke began again to run, his lungs aching from it. Too many cigars, he thought.

He passed the first block, running across the intersecting street; he then passed broken store windows, a mailbox knocked over apparently by a car in haste to evacuate the city, a fire hydrant with the caps off and a few drops of water still dribbling from it. He reached the next interesection, glanced down it to make certain Soames wasn't suckering him, hadn't doubled back. Then he ran down the next block.

There was a broad expanse of burnt-out lawn, a Baptist church at the far end, the church untouched. Rourke stopped a moment, catching his breath, staring at the church. "Why wasn't it vandalized?" he asked himself aloud, then shook his head and began to run again, reaching the end of the block.

There was one more block to go before the street down which Soames had turned. Rourke, his arms out at his side again, ran it dead out, half collapsing against the side of the corner building—a real estate development firm—then peering around the corner.

Rourke's heart sank a moment. Soames was nowhere in sight, but at the end of the street, approximately two blocks down, was an uncharacteristically elaborate athletic field and stadium.

Rourke stared at it. The stadium looked to have cost more than all the other buildings in the town combined.

Rourke reached up under his left armpit, snatching one of the twin Detonics pistols from the Alessi shoulder holsters. He thumbed back the hammer, pushing up the frame-mounted thumb safety. Bending into his stride, he began to run again, hugging the side of the buildings he passed, getting across the alley, then to the next street and into the next block. He slowed, the athletic field less than two hundred yards away; and beyond the cinder track, with some of the painted white lines in the field still visible, was the stadium.

Something inside Rourke told him Soames was there. The wind was blowing cold again. He pulled the waist-length brown leather jacket back on. Then, at a slow trot, started across the athletic field, snatching the second Detonics from under his right arm into his left hand, thumbing back the hammer and crooking his thumb around to push up the safety.

Rourke stopped beside the stadium entrance, examining the dust on the concrete surface, a smile crossing his lips. Faintly, he could detect a tire tread in the blown sand.

Rourke started through the entranceway, and as he

reached the end of the long tunnel, he scanned the bowl of the stadium itself, squinting against the sunlight despite the dark glasses he wore. A smile crossed his lips again. Apparently the games held at the stadium had once been broadcast over local radio. There was a low-gain antenna beside the booth on the far, topside of the arena, the sort of antenna that could be used to transmit to a more powerful receiver-sender fifty miles or so away.

There was no sign of Soames or his bike.

Rourke walked up the low, broad concrete steps into the grandstand, then started along the circumference of the stadium toward the booth and the antenna.

One Detonics .45 in each hand, Rourke moved slowly ahead, looking from side to side. He no longer cared if Soames detected his presence—because there was nowhere the spy could go. Soames could smash his radio, but that was unlikely. Rather than going cold, out of contact with his Soviet masters, he'd likely try to make a fight of it. Perhaps Soames had weapons stashed somewhere in the stadium; perhaps there had been a weapon concealed on his body—a holster that carried a snubby revolver or medium frame auto in the top of his cowboy boot. It didn't matter, Rourke thought.

Rourke stopped halfway around the stadium, beside the broadcast booth. The antenna was corroded, weather-stained, but a new-looking, almost shiny coax cable ran from it, through what seemed to be a freshly drilled hole in the concrete below the grandstand.

Rourke turned around, his eyes searching for the nearest steps down into the stadium complex beneath the stands. He found them, then started walking toward them. He stopped at the head of the steps, looking at the twin pistols in his hands, holding them as if weighing them.

Both pistols in front of him, elbows tucked close at his sides—he thought if he could see himself he'd be reminiscent of a cowboy in a silent picture—he started down the steps, into the darkness of the shadow there.

Rourke stopped halfway down the steps. With the back of his right hand he pushed the sunglasses up off the bridge of his nose and into his hair. He started walking again.

Rourke stopped, his left foot on the last step, his right foot on the concrete walkway of the tunnel. He held his breath, listening. Voices. He heard two voices, the words unintelligible but distinct enough that Rourke could tell they were in English. They were coming from the farthest end of the tunnel.

Rourke began walking, hugging his body against the rough concrete wall, the pistol in his right hand held high, the one in his left held flat along his left thigh.

He could hear the voices more clearly. He stopped, seeing the darker blackness of the new coax cable leading down from above, then snaking ahead into the shadow along the tunnel and toward its end. Rourke shifted the Detonics in his right hand into his belt, taking the sunglasses off his head, putting them in their case under his coat. His right fist clenched around the pistol again and he moved slowly, cautiously ahead.

The voices were clear enough now to be understood, at least in part. One of them belonged to Soames: "I don't care, Veskovitch. Why worry? All that damned earthquake is going to do is kill more Americans and kill a bunch of them danged Cubans. I don't think your folks give a shit about them anyway."

156

"You were wise to come," the other voice—Vesko-vitch, Rourke assumed—began. "But you are wrong. We must contact headquarters. This is an important development. There may be valued Soviet personnel working in Florida at this very moment. They at least must be gotten out. It is not your responsibility, nor is it mine, to determine who should live and die. You speak of a disaster which could take millions of lives. Do you wish this on your conscience?"

Rourke, standing in the darkness along the wall, smiled. The Soviet agent, probably KGB, was sound-ing almost humanitarian. Soames sounded like a bloodthirsty animal. Rourke moved ahead, more slowly now, cautiously, not being able to see more than six feet ahead into the shadows.

He stopped, holding his breath, cursing mentally, then reached down and rubbed his right shin. There had to be a ramp down into the tunnel. He had just bumped his shin against Soames's motorcycle. Rourke shoved the Detonics from his right hand into his trouser band, then using the Safariland stainless hand-cuff key from his key ring, he found the valve stem on the rear tire and deflated it. He didn't want Soames using the bike for a getaway.

Pocketing the key ring, Rourke snatched the Detonics from his belt again. A pistol in each hand once more, he sidestepped the bike, then pressed against the concrete tunnel wall and moved ahead again.

The voices were louder now. "Well, go on then and call Varakov or whoever gets it—but let 'em know I brought it to you."

"You are still worried General Varakov will come for you, perhaps sometime in the middle of the night, and kill you for molesting a child. He did not like you. You were afraid of him and he knew that."

"Shut up," Soames snapped.

Rourke took two steps ahead, into the small cone of yellow light from the niche in the tunnel wall just ahead, then turned, both guns leveled, looking into the tiny room.

"I'll go along with that, Soames—but you two shut up," Rourke whispered, the safety catches down on both pistols as he aimed one at Soames and one at Veskovitch.

"Who—"

"Move and I kill you," Rourke interrupted.

Soames started for the radio, a move Rourke hadn't anticipated from the paramilitary commander. Rourke fired the Detonics in his right hand, the slug tearing into Soames's left side, kicking the man back against the far wall.

But Veskovitch was coming toward him, a pistol in his right hand, the gun firing.

Rourke fired the Detonics in his left hand, but Veskovitch was already on him, the 185-grain .45 ACP slug tearing into Veskovitch's left leg. There was a loud cry of pain and anguish. The pistol in Veskovitch's right hand discharged and Rourke could feel heat against his own left hand, glancing down to it, as he smacked the .45 in his right down across the KGB man's neck. There was no wound in the hand, but the bullet had passed close, Rourke realized, perhaps just barely grazing his skin.

The Russian's left fist was circling upward and Rourke's right forearm blocked it. The Russian was screaming, "The radio, Soames—smash it!"

His left knee smashing up into the Russian's

gunhand, Rourke looked over the KGB man's back. He could see Soames staggering away from the far wall, a pistol in his right hand aimed at the radio.

Rourke tried bringing his right hand into position to shoot, but the Russian grappling with him shoved against him and the .45 discharged into the concrete over their heads, the slug ricocheting maddeningly off the concrete walls. Rourke backhanded the Detonics in his left hand across the KGB man's face, knocking him away.

Then Rourke brought down the Detonics pistol in his right hand, raising the left one into position as well, both pistols discharging simultaneously, both slugs driving into Soames's center of mass. The Texas commander fell back, the Detective Special .38 in his right hand discharging into the floor at his feet.

The echo of the gunshots still reverberating in the tiny room, almost deafeningly, Rourke wheeled right. The KGB man was raising his pistol to fire.

No time to swing his guns on line, Rourke hurtled himself sideways toward the Russian. Both Rourke's pistols clattered to the floor as his left hand reached for the KGB man's gunhand, his right hand going for the throat.

The agent's pistol discharged and for the first time, his ears ringing with the sound, Rourke noticed it—a Detonics .45, like his own, but blued. Rourke's left hand on the KGB man's wrist, he slammed the gunhand down, the pistol firing again.

Rourke moved his hand from the Russian's throat and smashed his right fist across the man's jaw.

The Russian's head snapped back and Rourke moved up on his haunches, straddling the KGB man's body. He studied the eyes—the lids were closed, not

159

fluttering. Rourke, prying the man's fingers from the blue Detonics .45 then, bent low, trying to feel for breath. Rourke touched his fingers to the Russian's neck, then to the man's wrist. He raised the head slightly. However he'd hit the man, the neck had snapped and the Russian was dead. He hadn't wanted that.

Rourke thumbed up the safety on the blue Detonics and rammed the pistol into his belt, intending to keep it. He found his own pistols, then walked the few steps to Soames. Despite three hits from Rourke's .45s, the paramilitary leader was still breathing.

Gently, Rourke rolled Soames over. The wounds would make him die, but not for several minutes if his constitution were strong, Rourke determined. "Soames, how do you make your contacts?"

"Go to hell . . ."

Rourke thumbed down the safety on the Detonics in his right hand, touching the muzzle to the traitor's left cheekbone. Almost softly, Rourke told him, "I can either let you die comfortably or painfully, Soames. You know I'm a doctor. I've got a small emergency kit under my coat," Rourke lied. "I can give you a shot." There was an emergency kit with syringes, but back on his bicycle. "Morphine? Sound good? You could linger for hours," Rourke lied again. He thumbed up the safety on the Detonics and shoved it in the holster under his left armpit, then did the same on the second pistol, placing it in the holster under his right arm.

As if he were uncaring, Rourke took the blue Detonics that had belonged to the KGB man and studied it, dumping the half-spent magazine, clearing the chamber. The pistol was in pristine condition, still wearing the original checkered walnut grips. He made a mental note to check the body and the room for spare magazines which were interchangeable with his own guns.

"Well?" Rourke studied Soames's face—it was white, drained. Soames had a few minutes at most to live and Rourke hoped Soames didn't know it. "Die in pain or get the morphine shot?"

"Gimme the shot," Soames grunted.

"The radio first. Tell me how to make the contact. I try it, it works, then the shot."

"All right, all right," Soames said through gritted teeth. "Songbird to Condor One, request—request relay." Soames coughed.

"What relay?" Rourke asked, trying to keep his voice calm. Blood spurted from Soames's mouth when he coughed.

"Request—relay—nineteen. Gets you—"

"Through," Rourke finished, then bent over Randan Soames, thumbing the lids on the dead eyes closed.

Rourke stood up. He walked over to the radio and flicked it on. He assumed they were using English on the radio—that way, if the signal were intercepted it would attract less attention. Rourke picked up the microphone, staring at it a moment, then at the men to whom the radio had been so important. "Songbird to Condor One," he called. "Requesting relay nineteen, over."

In a moment the radio crackled and there was a voice. "Relay nineteen through to Condor One—stand by."

Rourke lit one of his small cigars. He had no intention of going anywhere.

Chapter 34

"Harmon maybe is doin' the right thing," Mary Beth muttered, her eyes seemingly focused on the fire in the center of the cave floor.

"What do you mean?" Sarah Rourke asked, naked under her blanket, trying to warm herself and rid her bones of the chill they'd felt ever since the swim that previous night.

"With goin' up to Canada—all our men are gonna be dead by tomorrow afternoon. Some Army Intelligence fella that brings us supplies was out and left just before you and Harmon got here. He says the execution is on for tomorrow. To show the Resistance what'll happen if they keep up fightin'."

Sarah sat there silently like the rest of the women in the cave. Harmon Kleinschmidt was sleeping farther back in the cave in what seemed like an additional chamber. Some of the women were half undressed, apparently none of them worried that Harmon would wake up and see them. Sarah huddled in her blanket. "Aren't you going to try to do something to save your husbands, your boyfriends?" she asked finally.

"Like what, lady?" Mary Beth asked her, staring up and across the fire into Sarah's eyes.

"Like," Sarah paused, "like a rescue attempt." Sarah concluded lamely.

"Kleinschmidt can't do nothin'. He's gonna be laid up for a long time."

"Well, we don't necessarily need a man to do it. We could do it ourselves."

"We?" Mary Beth asked.

"Well, I meant the women—not me personally. Women *could* rescue them; you don't need a man to lead you."

"You volunteerin'?" Mary Beth's smile was something Sarah didn't like.

"Well, I don't really know any—"

"What I thought. Wind is all," Mary Beth snapped, looking back into the fire.

Sarah Rourke could feel her cheeks getting hot. Perhaps a fever, she thought—from the cold of the water. But maybe something else, she realized.

"All right," Sarah said, her voice low, so soft she could almost barely hear it herself. "All right," she said again, louder. "I'll do it. If you need someone to lead it, I'll do it."

"What?"

"I'll do it," she said, standing up, catching at the blanket and pulling it around her. She felt foolish suddenly and started toward the far end of the cave to find dry clothes. It was no time to lounge around talking with the girls. Somehow that made her feel more foolish now. "I'll do it," she said again without bothering to turn around. She wished, silently, that she knew how.

Chapter 35

Rourke sat at the radio, speaking slowly into the microphone, "This is John Rourke. Tell General Varakov I want to speak with him. It's important, more important than he could realize."

Rourke stopped talking, listening to the static on the receiver. Then there was a voice, barely audible in the transmission, because it was at low power and relayed several times, bad as well. "One moment." The air went dead. Rourke waited, stubbing out his cigar, then lighting another one, rolling the dark tobacco into the left side of his mouth. He studied the receiver. It was powered by storage batteries and these were charged, apparently, by a foot-powered tredle off in the corner.

"This is Varakov. Rourke?"

"This is Rourke, General. Can we speak freely?"

There was a pause for a moment. He wondered if Varakov thought that perhaps he had called to discuss the death of Karamatsov which both Varakov and Rourke had caused.

"I suppose so," Varakov said. Rourke remembered the voice from the time in Texas, as he had rescued Chambers and forced Karamatsov to walk him out.

"I have what I think you will agree is grievous news—and, frankly, I need your help," Rourke began.

There was a long pause, then: "My help?"

Rourke simply said, "Yes, because I think I understand you, and I respect you. I need your help."

There was another long pause, then the tired voice came over the static of the speaker. "Tell me this thing, Rourke. I will only promise to listen."

"Agreed, sir," Rourke said slowly. He started at the beginning, how he had rescued Sissy Wiznewski from the Brigands, what she had told him regarding the artificially created fault line that would very soon precipitate the earthquake which would sever Florida from the U.S. mainland, about the hundreds of thousands of lives that would be lost. Finally, before he concluded, Rourke added, "Maybe I have you figured wrong, but I don't think so. Can you help?"

There was a long silence, and for a moment Rourke thought something had gone wrong with the transmission. "This is all true—you give me your word on this thing?"

"To the best of my knowledge, General, yes."

"You have seen this seismographic evidence with your own eyes?"

"One sheet. The rest was lost with her bike."

"You are a man of science. This is possible?"

"I think so," Rourke admitted.

"You ask that I make a truce, between your U.S. II forces and the Soviets?"

"Temporary, of course."

"Of course. What about the Cubans? You seriously

think that they will believe you—or me?"

"If we can get them to take it seriously enough, they'll evacuate themselves I suppose. Then your people and mine can move in and evacuate the civilians."

"Why should I do this thing?"

"I don't know," Rourke said honestly, staring at the speaker above the radio as if he could somehow see Varakov's face in it. "I don't know," Rourke repeated.

"But you think that I will?"

"Yes. If you can, I think that you will."

"Natalia is there, on a mission with Colonel Miklov to negotiate with the Cubanos over a few minor difficulties. I can contact her, have her break the news to the Cuban commander. But you must do two things."

"What?" Rourke said slowly.

"I think this woman—Wiznewski with the strange first name—must go to Florida, show the piece of paper, talk to the Cuban commander. And perhaps you should go, too. If this is necessary, you promise me that you will not board a plane to evacuate until Major Tiemerovna has boarded as well? Agreed?"

"Why do you say that?"

"She will stay to help in the evacuation—you know that."

"I suppose Natalia would," Rourke commented into the microphone, his mind suddenly filled with her image—the dark hair, the bright blue eyes, the softness of her, the courage, too. "Yes, she would. I agree. I do not leave without her. And I suppose it would be necessary for the girl to go there. But as soon as they are convinced, I must get put in contact with your emergency commanders and the Cubans. My friend

Paul Rubenstein is in Florida now. I'm not certain exactly where."

"The Jew? I think I know. We thought at first it was you." Varakov outlined to Rourke a Soviet intelligence report on a single-handed attack on a Cuban detention camp. The young man had fought "like a lion," and most of the internees at the camp were Jews. "It must be Rubenstein. Yes, we will help you to find him—in exchange for your shepherding Major Tiemerovna."

"She was a Captain," Rourke said.

"I promoted her—for bravery. You understand?"

Rourke smiled, wishing for a moment he could see the old man's face, wondering what it looked like now. Were the eyes sad, was there still humor there?

"Yes, General. How do we contact each other? I can bring this radio to headquarters with me."

There was a pause. "Yes. I would speak with this Mr. Chambers and arrange the details of the truce. Did you—"

Rourke smiled. "Soames? The child molester? Did I kill him?"

"Yes . . . I assume . . ." The voice trailed off.

"Your man Veskovitch was very brave and died well. If he had a family—" Rourke let the sentence hang.

"I will see that they know. Good-bye for now, Rourke." The radio went dead. Rourke sat there by the yellow light, not saying anything, not thinking anything. There was a picture now, vivid in his mind, and he almost wanted it to go away. It was an indefinite and changing picture. Sometimes a face, sometimes a way of standing or walking—and sometimes, if a voice could be pictured, it was a voice. Natalia. They were to meet again, he knew.

Chapter 36

"The fact is, General Santiago, that if these misdirected actions of your line commanders near the border continue, it will do nothing to further the cause of harmonious relations between your people and ours," Miklov said in perfect Spanish. Then he leaned back from across the table, seemingly studying the Cuban commander's face across the highly polished wood separating them.

Natalia had played tennis often before the Night of the War. But she had always more enjoyed watching it well-played by two worthwhile adversaries. As she turned her head now to look at Santiago, she felt a similar feeling. It was up to Santiago either to volley the ball Miklov had served or lose the match.

"But according to the reports of my line commanders, Colonel Miklov, there have been no such incidents beyond the course of normal patrolling or pursuit of an escaping Resistance fighter and the like.

There have been no intentional incursions into your country's space."

Natalia looked back at Miklov, smiling. "But General Santiago must realize that whatever the cause for border incursions, that again they do little to promote harmonious relations. It is my hope that such incursions can be stopped completely and this is my purpose here—to discuss these matters and work out a mutually equitable solution."

• Natalia began to turn to Santiago, but then her eyes drifted across the room to a white-coated, dark-skinned steward entering the room. The man stopped beside Santiago and placed a silver tray on the table before him. Santiago unfolded a note on the tray, nodded to the steward, and returned the note to the tray. The steward picked up the tray and left. Santiago looked at her a moment, then said, "My dear Major Tiemerovna, there is a radio-telephone message for you. You may take it on the telephone in your room if you wish."

"Thank you." Natalia stood and both Santiago and Miklov began to rise. "Please, gentlemen," she murmured, sweeping past the end of the table and touching the fingers of her left hand to Santiago's epauletted shoulder as she walked by.

Natalia crossed the room, feeling Santiago's eyes on her, then opened the double doors and walked through the doorway, closing them behind her. She leaned against the door a moment, looking down at the carpet beneath her feet. The caller had to be Varakov, she knew. She pushed away from the door and started toward the stairs, running up to the second floor of the house, then to the door of her room, quickly opening it. She walked inside and closed the door behind her. Sitting on the edge of the bed, smoothing her skirt under her, she lifted the telephone receiver, pulling off an earring as she brought the earpiece up. "This is Major Tiemerovna," she said into the receiver.

"Natalia, listen carefully," her uncle's voice began. "Rourke called me—the news he had was important. He used one of our own radio receivers. That is not important, though. Listen carefully."

Natalia looked down at her lap, then past the hem of her light blue skirt, along her bare legs and to her feet, then along the blue carpet and toward the glass doors leading onto the balcony and past the open curtains. She could just see the ocean beyond. "John Rourke," she whispered into the telephone. She heard her uncle telling her of the impending destruction of Florida, the meeting she had to arrange under a flag of truce for Rourke and the Wiznewski woman with General Santiago. She heard all of it, but the words that most stayed with her were, "John Rourke." She would see him again. . . .

For several minutes after the conversation with her uncle she lay back across the bed. It was incredibly new to her, the idea that she could love someone and yet debate whether or not she should try to kill him.

Chapter 37

"I don't know what the hell you're talkin' about, fella," the red-faced, beer-bellied man told Rubenstein, then turned back to work on his boat.

"Captain Reed gave me your name, Tolliver. He said you were the man down here."

"I don't know no Captain Reed. Now get out of here!"

Paul Rubenstein, the sun glaring down on him, his legs tensed, realized then he'd been balling his fists opened and closed. He reached out with his left hand and grabbed the florid-faced Tolliver by the left shoulder and spun him around, his right fist flashing out and catching the larger man at the base of the chin, the man falling back across the front of his boat.

Tolliver pushed himself up onto his elbows, squinting at Rubenstein. "Who the hell are you, boy?"

"I told you," Rubenstein said, his voice low. "My name is Paul Rubenstein. I'm just a guy who needs your help. I know Captain Reed of U.S. II. He gave me your name when I told him I was coming down here. Now you're bigger than I am, probably stronger, but believe me, I can be meaner—I learned since the Night of the War. Now," Rubenstein shouted, "I need your help!"

"Doin' what?"

"You ever go down by the camp—the big one?"

"Maybe."

"I'm going to break everybody out of there—and you're going to help me."

"You're full of shit, boy."

Rubenstein glanced over his shoulder, saw no one by the sandy cove where he'd found Tolliver working on his beached boat. Then Rubenstein reached under his leather jacket and pulled out the Browning High Power, shoving the muzzle less than two inches from Tolliver's nose. The hammer went back with an audible double click. "If you can sleep nights seeing those people in there, then whatever I could do to you would be a favor. You either help me round up some people in the Resistance to get those folks out of there, or I'm killing you where you stand."

"You're the one caused all that fracas there this morning, ain't you?"

Rubenstein nodded, then said, "Yeah—I am."

"Put the gun away. Why the hell didn't you say so in the first place. I'll help, then we can all get ourselves killed together. Never fancied much dying alone, if you get my drift."

Rubenstein raised the safety on the Browning and started to shift it down when there was a blur in front of his eyes. Tolliver's right fist moved and Rubenstein fell back into the sand, starting to grab for his gun.

"Now take it easy, fella. That was just to make us even. You shoot me, and you'll never find the Resistance people."

And Tolliver's big florid face creased into a smile, and he stuck out his right hand.

Rubbing his jaw with his left hand, Rubenstein looked at the bigger man—then they both started to laugh.

Chapter 38

Rourke opened the hatch on the DC-7 and looked out across the airfield. He could tell General Santiago by the ensignia on the collars of his G.I.-style fatigues; but the only face Rourke recognized was that of Natalia. He looked at her eyes, saw the recognition there and then threw down the ladder.

"Come on, Sissy," he said to the girl standing a little behind him.

Rourke started down the ladder to the runway, helping the girl. As Rourke turned to start across the field toward Santiago and Natalia, he stopped, his hands frozen away from his body, frozen in the movement of sweeping up toward the twin Detonics pistols under his coat. There was a semicircle of men, Cuban soldiers, with AK-47s in their hands, their muzzles pointed at him.

Rourke looked beyond the emotionless faces of the soldiers and across the airfield. Santiago seemed to be poorly disguising a smile—but Rourke couldn't read Natalia's eyes. There was a command shouted by Santiago, the words something Rourke recognized. "Arrest that man. Seize that woman and the airplane and its pilot—immediately!"

Rourke cocked his head slightly toward Natalia as she took Santiago's arm, hugging it to her it seemed. Her eyes just stared ahead. Coldly, Rourke thought.

"What's happening?" Sissy Wiznewski asked, her voice low, trembling.

Rourke reached out—watching the soldiers watching him—and took her hand, saying to her, "I'll let you know as soon as I find out myself. It wasn't Natalia's way, Rourke thought—not to go against her uncle's wishes, not to use the Communist Cubans as an instrument for her own revenge.

He tried to read the woman's face from the distance separating them. He'd been told there was a Colonel Miklov there with Natalia. But he saw no Russian officer, not even someone in civilian clothes.

A man Rourke judged as a squad leader stepped toward him, saying in bad English, "I will take your guns."

Rourke again glanced toward Natalia—nothing. He decided to gamble, reaching slowly under his coat with first his left, then his right hand, taking the Detonics pistols and handing them butt first to the squad leader. Since the man hadn't asked for his knife, Rourke didn't volunteer it.

"You will come with me," the man said. Rourke started to walk ahead, still holding Sissy's hand. "The woman—she will see the general."

Rourke eyed the soldier, then looked over the man's

shoulder toward Natalia. He thought he caught an almost imperceptible nod. But it could have been his imagination, or wishful thinking he thought. He gambled again. "Sissy, it'll be all right, I think. Just do a good job convincing the general that the quakes are real. Don't worry," he added. Then Rourke let go of her hand and started ahead, the soldiers falling in ranks around him. He saw the squad leader from the corner of his eye, handing the twin Detonics pistols to Santiago. Rourke saw Natalia looking down at the guns in Santiago's hands, saw her lips move, saying something. Then Santiago—with almost ridiculous formality, Rourke thought—bowed and offered the pistols to Natalia. She took them, smiling, and for the first time he could hear her.

Natalia was laughing.

Chapter 39

Paul Rubenstein looked across the hood of the jeep, then at the florid-faced Tolliver beside him behind the wheel. "That's a death camp," Rubenstein said slowly, staring now past the hood of the jeep and to the lower ground and the road and the camp beyond it.

"The commandant has a reputation for being anti-Jewish."

"They put an anti-Semite in charge of a detention camp in an area with a large Jewish population," Rubenstein interrupted. "Then they know what's going on, the Communist Cuban government."

"Some say the commandant down there, Captain Guttierez, dislikes the Jews almost as much as the anti-Castro Cubans. He's been exterminating every one of them he can find."

"Why have you waited to do something?" Rubenstein asked him.

"Simple—you'll see in a minute—look." And Tolliver

pointed over his shoulder.

Rubenstein, his palms sweating, turned around and looked behind the jeep. Tolliver's number-one man, Pedro Garcia, a free Cuban, had gone to get the rest of the Resistance force. Rubenstein's heart sank. Two men approximately his own age, a woman of about twenty and a boy of maybe sixteen.

Tolliver, his voice lower than Rubenstein had heard it before, sighed hard. "That's why, Rubenstein. Two men, a woman, a boy, me, and Pedro—that's it. Now you. You still want to do this thing?"

Rubenstein turned around in the jeep's front passenger seat, stared down over the hood toward the camp. "Hell yes," he rasped, the steadiness of his own voice surprising him. "Yes I do."

Rubenstein felt the ground shaking, then looked at Tolliver. The man said, "Some little quakes like that have been coming the last week or so. Don't know why. This ain't earthquake country."

The trembling in the ground stopped and Rubenstein simply said, "Let's work out the details, then get started."

"We're gonna wait until dark, right?" Tolliver queried.

Rubenstein thought a moment. He'd learned from Rourke to trust your own vibes, your own senses and what they added up to, whatever the others felt. "No . . ." he began distractedly. "No—they won't expect an assault in daylight. I just don't think we've got the time to wait. We'll go soon."

Rubenstein was still watching the camp. He wondered how soon was soon enough.

Chapter 40

Natalia walked from her room and along the railing overlooking the first floor of the house. She stopped, staring at nothing, thinking of Rourke. Santiago had been easy to read. She smiled to herself. The Communist Cuban general had used Varakov's warning of the impending natural disaster, the coming of Rourke and Sissy Wiznewski—all of it as an excuse to see some sort of plot. For that reason when he had sent his men to arrest Colonel Miklov and Miklov went for a gun, she had disarmed Miklov and turned him over to Santiago. This action had pleased Santiago; *she* had pleased Santiago. That she despised him—mentally shrank from his touch, from his stare—was nothing of which the Cuban was aware. He thought, she knew, that somehow he thrilled her. And so—she smiled at the thought—she was free, still armed and able to move. Sissy Wiznewski was in Santiago's office trying to convince him of the reality of the massive quake.

Rourke and Miklov were imprisoned in the basement that had been converted to accommodate prisoners Santiago personally wished to interrogate—and to torture.

She smoothed her hands against her thighs, then reached down to the floor beside her booted feet for the large black purse. She opened it, then looked inside. Her own COP .357 Magnum four-shot derringer pistol, the two stainless steel .45 automatics Rourke habitually carried, her lipstick, and a change of under-wear—these items filled the bag.

Shrugging her shoulders, she turned from the railing and started down the stairs, smiling at the steward as he seemed to glide past Santiago's office doors. She stopped at the doors, the bag over her left shoulder, then knocked with her right hand. "It is Natalia, Diego," she said as sweetly as she could.

She heard an answering voice from inside, then opened the right-hand door and walked inside. Santiago stood, smiling. Sissy Wiznewski was already standing, the look on her face that of a schoolgirl who had just failed her most important final examination.

"This is all rubbish," Santiago pronounced with an air of authority. "This business of earthquakes is nothing more than a plot to cause us to evacuate Florida so Varakov's troops can invade here. You were wise to abandon your KGB friends and join us, my dear."

Smiling, she walked across the room, glancing at the seismic chart on the conference table, then at the frightened eyes of Sissy Wiznewski. "Yes," she murmured, reaching down and kissing Santiago's cheek as he sat down again.

As she drew her mouth away, she moved her left

hand upward, the COP pistol in it, pressing the muzzle against Santiago's left temple. "But, my General, it is true—and you will now do exactly as I say or the top of your head will soon decorate the ceiling above where you sit. For a small gun, I still have one of the most powerful .357 Magnum loadings in it—the 125-grain Jacketed Hollow Point. Do you know guns? A pity if you don't, but tests conducted for American police departments indicated this was perhaps the most effective .357 Magnum loading available. Want to see?"

Santiago turned his head slightly and she looked into his eyes, smiling. "You tricked me," he said.

"That, darling, should be obvious to even you," she cooed. "Now, you will call out to have Colonel Miklov sent up—immediately. The guards will wait outside the door for him. After Colonel Miklov arrives, I will free Rourke. Already, though, you will have issued orders to your commanders initiating the truce. And you will issue orders for the radio signal to be given that the U.S. II and Soviet planes may land, as well as issue orders to your line commanders to begin evacuating civilians. Including the concentration camp near the airport. Everyone. And, my dear Diego, if you are very good, you too can leave after everyone else has."

She looked at Sissy Wiznewski and asked matter-of-factly, "How soon?"

"The—the general said there had been some small earthquakes reported for the last five days around the area. I'd say it's a matter of hours, if that."

Natalia smiled at the girl, then turned back to General Santiago. "For your own sake, Diego, I sincerely hope there is enough time left."

She pressed the muzzle of the COP pistol tight against his head. "Make your first call, darling."

Chapter 41

"What the hell is going on down there?" Tolliver snapped, dropping to the ground behind a palm trunk, Rubenstein dropping down beside him, the Schmeisser in his right hand.

"It looks like they're getting out of the camp—but why? What's going on?" Rubenstein riveted his eyes to the camp. The guards were running from their posts; the officers were running too. Rubenstein looked overhead. Planes of every description imaginable were filling the sky from the west. "Those are American planes!"

"Commies use ones they found on the ground a lot."

"No—they're coming from the west, maybe Texas or Louisiana."

"You're dreamin' kid," Tolliver snapped.

"No! Look—more of them!" The droning sound in the air was as loud as anything Rubenstein could ever recall having heard. The sky was filled, the ground darkening under the shadows of the aircraft. The ground began to tremble under him, but this time more violently than before.

Rubenstein stood up, Tolliver trying to pull him down, the young man shaking away Tolliver's hand. "It's an earthquake. Some of those planes are landing." He looked down toward the camp. The Cuban guards and officers were fleeing, the gates of the compound wide open. "They're evacuating. There's gonna be an earthquake."

"You're nuts, kid."

Rubenstein looked down to Tolliver, started to say something, but then the ground shook hard and Rubenstein jumped away as a crack eighteen inches wide began splitting across the ground. Then a palm tree fell, just missing Pedro Garcia and the other Resistance people.

"A damned earthquake!"

As if to underscore Tolliver's shout, the ground began shaking harder, so hard Paul Rubenstein fell to the dirt on his hands and knees. "Oh my God!" he said.

Chapter 42

John Rourke sat in the detention cell, his feet up on the edge of the cot, his eyes focused on the guard sitting at the far end of the cell just beyond the bars. Rourke mentally shrugged. He'd waited long enough. He palmed out the A.G. Russell black chrome Sting IA with his left hand. He had not been searched.

"Guard," he rasped in English.

The Communist Cuban guard stood on the other side of the bars. "Si?"

"That's perfect," Rourke smiled. His left hand whipped forward, the Sting in his palm, point first, sailing from his hand, across the six feet or so to the wide bars, the shining black knife impacting square into the center of the guard's chest. Rourke was on his feet, diving toward the bars, his hands out, catching the guard before he fell and snatching the key ring. Rourke let the body fall to the basement floor as he reached around, fumbling for the right key. He found it and unlocked the cage, swinging the door out as far as it could with the body there, then going through.

He reached down, grabbing his knife, wiping the blade clean on the guard's uniform, then sheathing it. As he reached down for the Communist's AK-47, Rourke froze, a familiar voice behind him saying, "Wait, John!"

Rourke turned, slowly rising to his full height. His eyes tightly focused on Natalia, every outline of her tall, lithe body visible under the black jumpsuit she wore. And in her hands were his twin Detonics pistols, the hammers back.

"Well what is it? You going to kill me?"

"Why did you kill Vladmir?"

Rourke saw no reason to lie—to lie wasn't his way. "He was an animal, he would have killed you."

"My uncle told you this?"

"Yes." He hesitated. "But it was something I could see. Did he hurt you?"

"In many ways."

"Did I hurt you?"

"Only because you had no choice, because you have honor."

"I'm sorry," Rourke said softly.

The woman's eyes shifted a moment, down to her hands, then she took a small step closer to him, rolling over the pistols in her hands, presenting them butt first. "The earthquake—it has already started on the Gulf Coast. There is little time."

"I know," he told her, his voice low.

"Hold me, John—just for a moment. . . . Please."

The guns still in his hands, Rourke folded Natalia into his arms, feeling her dark hair against his stubbled

185

face. "I can't say everything will be all right, can I?"

"No," he heard the girl whisper. "Never lie to me, John. Then I would die, I think."

She stepped back from him, and he set the pistols down on the small table beside the cell door. It wasn't something he'd intended to do, he thought, even as he did it.

His hands grasped her by her elbows, then he drew her toward him, looking down into her eyes. Then he kissed her lips, his mouth crushing down on hers, her body pressed tight against him. As he held her, he could hear and feel her breathing. "I love you," she whispered.

Rourke started to open his mouth, but the woman in his arms touched her fingers to his lips. "No—" She said nothing else.

Rourke looked at her a moment, then smiled. "All right," he said slowly, then bent to pick up his guns. "You checked them?"

"Yes. There are five rounds in the magazine, one in the chamber. Just like you carry them."

Rourke left the pistols cocked and locked in his fists as he started away from the cell door, Natalia beside him in a moment with the dead guard's AK-47. "What's the situation?" he asked her as they reached the base of the stairs.

"Miklov—he is a good man—has my pistol to Santiago's head. I forced Santiago to begin the evacuation, and to begin the truce so our planes and yours can land. The girl, Sissy, is with Miklov. She will be safe."

Rourke turned and looked at Natalia, stopping in mid-stride. "Back there, I . . ."

"I understand you better than you think," she said, smiling a little.

"I know that," he told her, then started up the stairs two at a time.

Rourke kicked open the door into the main part of the house, the doorway leading into the hall. Men were running in every direction, armed men, servants, none of them giving Rourke and Natalia as much as a second glance. And suddenly below his feet, Rourke could feel the floor starting to shake. He glanced toward the high ceiling extending upward above the second floor. There was a chandelier there—crystal, Rourke thought absently. And suddenly it started to shake.

Rourke turned, pushing Natalia back into the basement doorway, shielding her with his body. The floor shook hard and there was a sound like an explosion as Rourke glanced behind him and toward the high ceiling. The chandelier crashed to the floor, shattering.

There was a gunshot then, loud but muffled, followed by a woman's scream.

Natalia looked up into Rourke's eyes. "That was Sissy—Santiago!"

The Russian girl was already running across the central hall, jumping to clear the debris of the chandelier, Rourke running behind her. She stopped in front of the double doors leading into Santiago's office, then lashed out with her left boot, the doors splintering apart. Rourke was beside her, shouldering through as she stepped into the doorway. They both stopped. Sissy Wiznewski was standing in the middle of the floor, her hands to her open mouth, her eyes wide. On the floor beside her were two men—one of them was Miklov, Rourke assumed. There was a knife sticking out, high in his chest, just below the throat. The second body belonged to Santiago. Rourke could tell from the uniform, but only that. Where the face had been there was now only a red, pulpy mass. There was a dark object in the center of the mass. Rourke had no idea what had happened to the other eye.

Chapter 43

Rourke dashed down the front steps of the house, the Detonics pistols in both hands firing into the Cuban troops in front of him. He dropped to one knee, snatching up an AK-47 from one of the dead soldiers, then bumping the selector to full auto and spraying the Soviet-built assault rifle ahead of him, hearing Natalia opening up beside him. "The half track—there!" Rourke shouted, starting down the steps.

He could hear Natalia, behind him now, screaming to the Wiznewski girl, "Sissy, get those guns and ammunition belts—hurry!"

Rourke reached the truck, snapping the butt of the AK-47 up into the jaw of a Communist Cuban soldier hanging onto the running board. Then he climbed up, into the cab, reloading the Detonics pistols and leaning the AK-47 beside him against the seat. He turned the key, the half-track truck's engine rumbling to life. "Come on!" he shouted.

Natalia backed her way down the steps, firing the AK-47 in witheringly accurate three-round bursts as the Cubans started after her. Rourke swung open the cab door, snatching the AK-47 from beside him, half-stepping out onto the running board. He fired the assault rifle, nailing two Cuban soldiers running up for Natalia from her left flank. "Come on!"

Sissy Wiznewski, her arms laden with rifles, belts with spare magazines festooned around her shoulder, was stumbling toward the truck. Rourke jumped to the driveway, feeling the ground tremble under his feet.

He grabbed an armful of the guns and pushed the girl up into the truck cab.

As Rourke turned, shouting again to Natalia, "Now! Come on!" he looked up. The sky overhead was dark, almost green in color, and he could feel rain on his face.

He looked down, firing a burst from the AK-47, Natalia beside him now. "Get into the cab. We have to make it to the airfield—come on!"

He shoved Natalia in, climbing back behind the wheel. The door still open, he released the emergency brake, gunning the engine as he let out the clutch. The half-track lurched ahead along the gravel drive.

The cab door slammed as Rourke cut the wheel into a hard right, a truck blocking his path. He took the half-track up over a small rock barrier and onto the lawn of the estate, then across it, Natalia firing out the opposite window. He could hear the Russian coaching the Wiznewski girl in how to change magazines for the AK-47s. Rourke cut the wheel hard left, shouting, "Hold on!" He turned the truck from the grass and back onto the gravel driveway, toward the closed iron grillwork gates at the far end. The shaking of the ground was something inescapable now—he could feel it even as the half-track lurched ahead.

Rourke fumbled for the windshield wiper switch.

The rain was starting to fall in sheets now. The double iron gates were just yards ahead and Rourke, double-clutching to upshift and get some speed, shouted to the women, "Get your heads down—we're going through!"

Less than a yard from the gates the brick support columns began to crumble as the ground running along side the driveway started to crack. Rourke hammered his right foot down on the accelerator, released, double-clutched, and upshifted, then stomped the accelerator again. The crack in front of them widened. He had no choice but to drive over it.

He could feel the front tires go into the crack, hear the engine groaning, then feel the half-track bump and lurch ahead. He stomped down hard on the gas pedal as the front of the truck smashed into the gates, the brick support columns already crumbling down on the cab, the windshield cracking across its entire length.

The gates split open and Rourke cut the wheel into a sharp right along the road paralleling the estate. He glanced to his right at Natalia, her hair streaming rain water as she leaned from the cab window firing at their pursuers.

He could see the crack in the ground widening and running alongside them now, seeming to move faster than they were.

"I've got to outrun that fissure!" Rourke shouted over the roar of the engine and the howling of the wind and rain. "Natalia, get back inside!" Rourke lessened his pressure on the gas pedal, worked the clutch and shifted into fourth, the engine whining. He shot a glance to his right. He was gaining on the widening fissure in the earth; but silently he wondered if he could pass it before it cut the road ahead of him and blocked his only chance of escape—the airfield ten miles away.

Chapter 44

Sarah Rourke could just see the faces of her children, Michael and Annie, in the back of the fisherman's boat, packed there with Harmon Kleinschmidt, two of the women, and the dozen or so other children. Sarah had reasoned that once the attack against the Soviet prison compound had taken place, the island would no longer be safe. Mary Beth had surprisingly, she thought, agreed with her.

Mary Beth was at the wheel of the boat Sarah had stolen earlier, taking it coastward. And again, Sarah smiled at the thought, she was wearing borrowed clothing. She had reasoned that the best way to reach the prison and free the men who were to be executed that day was to appear as innocuous as possible. Most of the women were wearing dresses; some of them, herself included, had bundles wrapped up to look like babies. Inside Sarah's was a borrowed MAC-10 .45 caliber submachine gun. Under the long, ankle-length skirt of the borrowed dress she wore, the .45 Colt automatic was strapped to her left thigh with elastic.

Mary Beth had beached the boat, and Sarah and the seven other women had fought their way through the surf. The tides were high, and the wind strong for some reason. From the shore there had been a two mile walk into town, and at Sarah's urging the women had split up into three groups to attract less attention to themselves and to avoid blowing the entire operation should one group be captured.

Now, as Sarah rocked the imaginary baby in her arms a half-block from the factory gates—the factory that was now a prison—she looked at the borrowed watch on her wrist. If a Soviet officer did not come along in another five minutes, she would have to scrap plan "A" as she called it and go to plan "B." The second plan called for an assault by herself and the rest of the women on the prison gates. It was suicide.

She sucked in her breath. There was a Soviet officer walking with a noncommissioned officer, turning into the street and walking toward her. She quietly wondered if she'd have the nerve. Still rocking the swaddled submachine gun in her arms, singing to it softly as she moved, she walked toward the Soviet officer.

She had no idea what rank he was, but since he was older-looking, she assumed the rank was high enough that his life would be important—she hoped so, at least.

She stopped, standing a few feet to the right and ahead of the Soviet officer and the soldier with him. "Sir?"

The officer stopped talking to the soldier, stopped walking and turned to face her. He nodded. "If you need help with your child, madam, there are doctors in the city who will offer what medical aid they can. The nearest facility is—" and he started to gesture down the block behind him.

"No, sir," Sarah told him, forcing a smile. "It isn't that. But it has to do with my baby. Please, would you look at him?" She hoped to appeal to the officer's vanity, to his ego. The helpless woman asking his advice—she hoped he saw it that way. She was committed now. There was little time before the execution was to take place.

The officer looked to the soldier beside him, shaking his head, saying something in Russian. "Very well, madam. But I fail to see . . ."

She started walking slowly toward him, watched the soldier's eyes, watched them shift as she moved her "baby" in her arms into a better position. The Soviet soldier started to open his mouth and Sarah swung the "infant" into position, letting the faded blue blanket fall to the ground at her feet. The MAC-10 swung in a firing position, the stubby muzzle aimed at the soldier, her right first finger twitching against the trigger, the soldier falling.

Sarah, her feet braced apart, turned the muzzle of the weapon against the officer, whispering, "I'll kill you too if you move."

There were soldiers running up from the prison gates, the gates open, and she turned back to the Soviet officer. "What is your name?"

"I am Major Borozeni."

"Major," she began, not attempting to pronounce the last name, "tell those soldiers to stop where they are and drop their guns, or you're dead."

The Russian officer smiled, beginning to laugh. "Madam, I am not so important that I can be used as any sort of bargaining—"

Sarah fired a burst into the cobbled street in front of the officer's gleaming boots, then looked up into his eyes. "For your sake you'd better be."

The major shouted something in guttural Russian and the soldiers stopped in their tracks. Sarah smiled at him. "See—you're more important than you thought. Doesn't that make you feel good?"

The Soviet major had ceased to smile.

"Let's go," she said. As the major began walking ahead of her in the direction in which she'd gestured with the submachine gun, the other women started coming from the doorways and alleys, their guns in their hands, advancing toward the Soviet soldiers and the open prison gates. Sarah's stomach churned. She had just murdered a man—for all she knew a good man, perfectly innocent, not trying to harm her.

She promised herself she would vomit later—there was no time now.

The soldiers parted in a wave in front of her, one of them moving and gunfire—from Mary Beth—cutting him down. "Nobody should try that again," Sarah screamed," or he gets killed!" Then, on second thought, she shouted to the major a few paces ahead of her, his hands upraised, "Major, repeat that in Russian. And remember that if anyone tries anything, you die first—I swear it." She heard the conviction in her own voice, realizing that she actually meant what she said.

The major passed through the gates, Sarah a few paces behind him. There were at least fifty Soviet soldiers there, all with guns, but Sarah kept walking.

The major said, "What is it you want, madam? Surely, you cannot—"

"You're right," she interrupted. "That's what I want. Those fifteen Resistance fighters. Get them out here, let them take arms, and we leave—nobody gets hurt."

The major stopped, not turning around, but looking over his shoulder at her. "You are insane!"

"Don't you forget it, either, Major," she told him, her voice trembling slightly.

"If you make it away from here alive, madam, I will find you," the major said, his voice velvety with hatred, she thought.

"You know you won't. If I thought that I'd kill you. Now give the orders."

"I—I cannot. I am not the commandant here."

"Give the orders—now!"

He looked at her again over his right shoulder, then just nodded.

The major shouted something in Russian. None of the soldiers moved. Then, his face reddening, he shouted again, louder. One soldier, then another started moving, and soon the ranks of Soviet soldiers opened and beyond them she could see the fifteen men, faces drawn, clothes torn and incredibly filthy. She listened as the major barked another command, then saw the first Russian soldier hand over his weapon to the Resistance man nearest him.

She almost fainted with relief. She shouted then, "No killing unless we have to!"

The haggard Resistance fighter turned, glared at her a moment, then lowered the muzzle of the rifle, just nodding. In a moment, the other fourteen men had armed themselves. "Order us a truck, Major," she told the officer still standing, hands up, in front of her.

"No!"

"Major, please. I'll kill you," she said softly.

He turned and looked over his shoulder at her again, then nodded. She heard him shouting in Russian, then in a moment heard the sound of an engine starting. She shouted, "Mary Beth, get everybody on board. Have them keep their guns trained on the courtyard here—and no shooting unless the Russians start it!"

She watched over the major's shoulders as the truck loaded, Mary Beth at the wheel.

Sarah said softly, "All right, Major, you come with us. Behave and you'll come out of this alive and unharmed. I promise."

He turned and looked at her. "And what if I do not?"

"This." She gestured with the muzzle of the submachine gun in her hands.

"Agreed," he almost whispered, his voice tight, as though he were about to choke on the words.

"Thank you." Sarah Rourke smiled.

In another two minutes, she judged, she and the major had boarded the truck, the major sitting between her and Mary Beth behind the wheel. She said to the major, "I know they'll follow us, but say something to make them follow at a distance. Tell them I'll kill you if I see anyone following us."

"Would you, madam?" he asked her.

"Of course," she said with a smile.

The major shouted in Russian and the Soviet troops by the gates fanned back. Mary Beth started the truck forward, then between the gates. It was starting to rain and Mary Beth had the windshield wipers going as the truck cleared the gates and turned into the street beyond. Then she cut a hard left into the intersection.

"Step on it, Mary Beth!" Sarah shouted.

"You'll never escape," the major told her, smiling.

"Better hope we do, Major," she answered, looking out the window behind her into the road. Whatever the major had said was working, she thought, and there were no Soviet vehicles in sight.

But she had learned well since the Night of the War. The Soviets were there, on parallel streets, waiting to make their move or calling in helicopters to keep the truck under observation. And now that she had gotten the fifteen Resistance men out of the prison, she felt a sick feeling in the pit of her stomach. She had no further plan—the rest of the way would have to be on guts and luck.

Chapter 45

Paul Rubenstein looked down at the ground below the low-flying aircraft. There were cracks in the ground—widening, it seemed, by the instant. Rain was falling in sheets and he silently prayed for the pilot. With Tolliver and Pedro Garcia and the others, Rubenstein had fought all the way to the airport, the other camps having spilled open as their Cuban Communist guards and warders had fled for their lives. Hundreds of men, women, and children were freed.

Many of the Cuban troops had fled by boat, the crafts visible as Rubenstein and the others had moved along the highway. Then Rubenstein had dropped off, going overland to retrieve his Harley, cutting back to the road again just ahead of the comparatively slow going convoy of every sort of land vehicle imaginable. Men hung on the outsides of the trucks, rode on the hoods of the cars and on the roof tops. It had taken two hours to reach the airport, and the airport itself was the greatest scene of mass confusion the young Rubenstein had ever witnessed. Cuban planes were loading Cubans, Soviet and American planes were loading the American refugees, some of the people from the camps having to be forced aboard the Soviet planes. The ground's trembling had been incessant, the cracks appearing everywhere in the runway surfaces.

And then Rubenstein had spotted Captain Reed, working to load one of the American planes impressed into the evacuation. Rubenstein had threaded his bike across the runways and buttonholed Reed, demanding to know what was happening.

And when Reed had told him, Rubenstein's heart sank. The tremors were the beginning of one massive quake that would cause the entire Florida Peninsula to separate from the rest of the Continental United States—what was left of it at least. Rubenstein had almost throttled Reed, demanding some kind of plane to get him to Miami where his parents were. Then Rubenstein had learned about Rourke. Rourke and the woman seismologist who had first brought the news of the impending disaster had gone to Miami to convince the Cuban commander of the reality of the impending disaster. Although Reed assumed they had been successful since the evacuation had been ordered, there had been no word from him since.

Again, Rubenstein had demanded a plane. Reed had agreed. There was a six passenger Beechcraft Baron specially altered to add almost another fifty miles per hour to its airspeed, the plane Reed himself had arrived in.

And now, as Rubenstein watched the ground cracking below the plane, watched the pilot manipulating the controls, and watched the sheets of rain, he wondered if by the time they reached Miami there would be a Miami to reach. Rourke was there, his mother and father were there. Even Natalia was there, Reed had told Rubenstein.

If Rourke died and he, Rubenstein, somehow survived, he would be honor bound, he knew, to continue the search for Rourke's wife, and the two children.

And what would he do, Rubenstein wondered, if the plane could land? Would he offload the Harley Davidson Reed and the pilot had grudgingly helped him get aboard? Would he somehow be able to find his parents, or John Rourke, or Natalia—but then simply die with them as the earthquake continued and the entire peninsula went under the waves?

A chill ran up Rubenstein's spine. It would be better to die—despite the chill, despite the sweating of his palms—than to live and never have tried to rescue the people— He stopped, a smile crossing his lips as he pushed his wire-framed glasses up on the bridge of his nose. "The people I love," he murmured softly.

Chapter 46

The main runway was beginning to crack. Rourke
snatched the young child from the refugee woman's
arms and handed the little girl aboard the DC-9, then
helped the woman to follow. He should never have let
Natalia go, he thought. They had reached the airfield,
the evacuation already under way and most of the
Cuban personnel aiding in the civilian evacuation or
too busy trying to save their own lives to offer resistance. Rourke and Natalia had gotten Sissy Wiznewski
on one of the first planes to take off after they had
reached the field, then Natalia had gone off to aid a
party of refugees, Rourke working with a Soviet
captain and an American major to bring some order to
the airfield and speed up the take-offs. More planes
hovered overhead, ready to land as they made a wide
circle of the field. It was a miracle that so far there had
been no mid-air collisions.

He loaded the last child aboard the aircraft, then the

little boy's crying mother, then slapped his right hand against the fuselage as the crewman by the door started closing up. Rourke snatched the borrowed walkie-talkie from his hip pocket. "Rourke to tower—DC-9 ready for take-off pattern!"

"Tower here. Roger on that."

Rourke shoved the radio into his pocket, then turned around scanning the field for Natalia. The rain was pouring down, and as the propellers of a plane passing along the runway near him accelerated, the rain lashed at Rourke's face. Pushing his streaming wet hair back from his forehead, he started to run, sidetracking a small, twin engine plane that was landing. He looked from side to side along the runway's length. There were more planes loading refugees at the far end of the field, and Rourke started running toward them. It was more than the promise he'd made Varakov, to see Natalia get away alive. But Rourke forced the thoughts from his mind as he ran on, sloshing through puddles on the runway, the wind blowing the rain at near gale force now, gusts buffeting his body as he dodged incoming and outgoing planes, making his way across the field.

Rourke reached the planes still loading, but Natalia was nowhere in sight. He grabbed a passing Soviet airman by the collar, shouting in Russian, "The Russian woman—where is she?"

The man looked uncomprehending a moment, a strong gust of wind lashing them both, catching the Soviet airman's hat and blowing it across the field. "Wait," the young man stammered. "A beautiful woman—dark hair, blue eyes?"

"Yes—where?" Rourke shouted over the wind.

"There, I think!" The airman pointed toward the

airfield control center, a complex of low buildings about five hundred yards away, nearer the water beyond the airfield than the runways.

Rourke started running, shouting over his shoulder, "Thank you!" but the young airman was already turned around, helping a woman load a baby aboard the nearest aircraft.

Chapter 47

They were out of the city and there was no sign of
Soviet pursuit. Sarah Rourke thought she knew why.
The ground under the truck was shaking, and the rain
was falling so heavily its color reminded her of staring
through a cheaply made plastic drinking glass. It was
almost impossible to see anything.

"Mary Beth! Stop the truck!"

The woman behind the wheel looked at her and hit
the brakes, the truck skidding slightly, then grinding to
a stop.

Sarah Rourke turned out the window and looked
into the rain again, then looked back at Mary Beth,
saying, "You want to get them into hiding, where that
fisherman took your children. But he was taking my
children up the coast so we could get away. I'm leaving
you now."

"You're crazy. You'll get killed out there alone."
Mary Beth called over the rain.

Sarah smiled. "No I won't."

She started out of the truck cab, the rain lashing at her, the long skirt of the dress plastered against her legs. "Get down!" she shouted to the Soviet major, gesturing with the MAC-10.

The man looked at her a moment, then started out of the truck. "What are you doing, Sarah?" Mary Beth screamed.

"I made this man a promise. I want to see it gets kept and nobody kills him."

There was a car coming down the highway—Russian, she thought. The car was swerving, the driver coming too fast in the rain. Sarah pressed herself against the side of the truck as the car skidded out of the oncoming lanes and across, narrowly missing the front of the truck and slamming into a utility pole.

Sarah gestured with the MAC-10 and the Soviet major ran beside her toward the car.

It was a recent, model, an American Ford. The two Soviet soldiers inside it were dead. She turned to the major. "Get the bodies out—and no funny business."

The Russian looked at her. "All right."

Sarah reached under her sodden dress, snatching the .45 automatic bound to her thigh, then cocking the hammer to full stand.

She pointed the gun at the major, the Russian clearing the body from the back seat and placing it beside the man already on the ground.

"Mary Beth—the gun!" Sarah held the MAC-10 out at arm's length in her left hand.

In a moment, Mary Beth was beside her. "You know what you're doin'?"

"Uh-huh," Sarah answered. "Good luck to you all.

Get out of here."

From the corner of her eye, she watched as Mary Beth ran back toward the truck, then climbed into the cab, the truck starting away.

Sarah turned and looked at the Major. "You've been wearing a pistol all this time, haven't you?" And she eyed the holster on his belt.

"Not very efficient of you, madam."

Taking a step closer to him, she said quietly, rain streaming down from her hair and across her face, "Take it out and toss it into the bushes."

"Yes," he answered, taking the gun slowly from the holster, eyeing her a moment, then tossing it away.

"Now get your shoulder to that car; get behind the wheel or something. I want it away from that pole."

"It will not drive, probably."

She started to speak, then the major interrupted her. "I know—I'd better hope that it drives."

The major slowly climbed behind the wheel of the car. There was a groaning noise, but then after several false starts, the engine turned over and she gestured to the major to back the car up. She kept the gun pointed at his head.

Sarah thought for an instant he was going to try to make a break, but the car stopped, and as she stepped back from the door he climbed out. "I can't believe it," he smiled. "Luck is with you today. The car drives."

"Now stand over there, by the utility pole," she ordered.

"For you to shoot me?"

"You'd better hope—" She stopped, hardly believing the sound coming from her own throat—laughter. The major was smiling, then he too began to laugh. He stepped back, slowly, still facing her and, as he reached the utility pole, she started into the car, behind the wheel.

"Madam!"

She looked into his face. He raised his right hand and saluted her, bowing slightly.

"To another campaign, madam!"

Sarah Rourke set the pistol down on the seat, put the gear selector into drive and started off the road shoulder, the rear wheels skidding in the mud. She could see the major, in the rearview mirror as she started onto the highway, still standing there in the rain beside the bent utility pole. The car sputtered, the windshield was cracked, and there was blood on the dashboard, but the car seemed to run adequately.

Silently, she hoped the major made it alive.

Chapter 48

Rourke reached the blown-open front doors of the terminal complex, kicking aside a huge shard of broken glass as he ran through the puddled doorway and inside. What was Natalia doing here? he asked himself. But as he turned the corner into the main hallway, there was no time to search his mind for an answer.

He stopped dead in his tracks. There were three dozen people in the room at the end of the hallway: men and women, some old, some Rourke's own age or so.

And Natalia was there, holding her tiny derringer pistol in her outstretched right hand. There were five Communist Cuban guards and one officer.

Rourke flattened himself against the wall of the corridor and inched ahead, trying to make something of the Spanish coming from inside the room. ". . . This is immaterial to me, senorita. Until a secure Cuban aircraft can be landed, these prisoners will remain with me. I do not care for the idea of shooting a KGB officer, even a self-proclaimed one. However, if you do not, for the last time, step aside and leave this room immediately, my men will open fire. If you care so much for these American military personnel and their wives, then I should think you would not wish to risk their being killed while my men are shooting at you."

Then Rourke's face creased into a smile. Natalia's quiet, alto voice, the Spanish perfect, began, "Captain, aside from the fact that I outrank you, I also will shoot you in the face if you do not order your guards to put down their arms. Many of these people, if they ever were American military personnel, are likely retired. There is no real American military any more. Any purposes you might have to interrogate these people do not take precedence over the humane purpose of allowing them to be evacuated before this entire airfield is torn to pieces. Now," she said as she gestured with the pistol, "stand out of my way or die!"

Rourke shook his head, stepping away from the corridor wall, firing one of the Detonics pistols into an overstudded chair midway between where he stood and the entrance to the room at the end of the hall. "Hold it—nobody moves!" he shouted in English, adding, *"Sus mannos arriba!"*

The Communist Cuban officer did just what Rourke had hoped, and turned to face his new challenger. As the captain moved, Natalia moved, the pistol in her hand flush against the side of the officer's head. "Now, Captain," Rourke snapped in English. "I believe the young lady asked you and your men to do something. Order your men to drop their guns. Now!"

Natalia, her voice low, in English this time, said, "Or I will kill you, Captain."

The captain didn't move for a long moment, Rourke holding both Detonics pistols on the five guards, their AK-47s still on line against him.

"Do as they say," the officer shouted in Spanish. The guards then, one by one dropped their rifles to the floor.

"Now the pistol belts," Rourke commanded.

The Cuban officer nodded, and his men began to drop their pistol belts to the floor.

"Natalia, take the Captain's pistol."

Rourke started forward, the floor beginning again to shake under him. Rourke, jostled to the corridor wall, pushed himself to the doors of the room, then stepped inside, the shaking of the floor more violent. He looked at the Communist Cuban officer and muttered, "If I had the time right now, I'd beat the shit out of you. You're going to wait for a Cuban plane to take you back with your prisoners. You think anybody out there cares if this whole peninsula goes into the sea? Can you imagine the tidal wave that'll hit Havana?"

Rourke backhanded the Cuban officer across the mouth with his left hand, the pistol jammed into his belt. "Idiot!" Rourke shouted.

"Come on," he said, starting the nearest of the refugees through the doorway. Then he turned to the Cuban guards, two of them holding up the officer, his mouth bleeding at the left corner. "You guys too—no sense dying!"

There was a white-haired older man near him and Rourke snatched up one of the AK-47s, saying, "Can you handle one of these, sir?"

"I sure can, son," the old man said, prodding the muzzle at the nearest guard.

There was a sudden violent shaking of the ground beneath them, the walls of the building and the floor under their feet beginning to crack. "Get out of here!" Rourke hollered, grabbing Natalia's hand and starting to run with her, the refugees behind them. Rourke, still holding Natalia's hand, turned the corner into the entrance hallway, the roof starting to cave in, Rourke bending into his stride and hitting the shattered doorway and running out onto the airfield. He shot a glance behind him, over his left shoulder. He could see the white-haired man, a woman with him, the rest of the refugees, and even the Cubans running for their lives.

Rourke scanned the runway from side to side. In the minutes spent inside the building, the volume of the rain had increased, the cracks in the runway surfaces had broadened, and all but a few of the planes had cleared the field. There seemed to be no more aircraft coming in for landing.

There was only one plane not in motion, the DC-3 Rourke and Sissy Wiznewski had originally landed in. Rourke recognized the markings. "Over there!" Rourke shouted, starting to run toward it, still holding Natalia by the hand, one of the Detonics pistols in his right fist. The rain was falling so heavily he could barely see as he ran. He heard Natalia scream, turned and saw her falling. He caught her, the ground beneath them shaking so violently that Rourke too almost lost his balance.

He let go of the Russian girl's hand. He and Natalia helped the older refugees, some of the Cuban guards

212

doing the same. The plane was still fifty yards away, Rourke gauged. And there was a crack, broadening almost imperceptibly, but expanding nonetheless. The crack was between them and the plane. Rourke started running again, helping an old woman across the field. There was only one plane on the field now, the DC-3, and one plane was landing. It was a twin-engine Beechcraft. Almost absentmindedly, Rourke noticed it from the corner of his right eye.

"Idiot," he thought.

The old woman started to collapse. Her cheeks were red with the exertion. Rourke jammed the Detonics into his belt beside the first gun, then swept the old woman up into his arms, running as best he could, jumping over the crack in the runway.

His feet sloshed through the deep puddles, the wind lashing the rain against his face. He heard himself shouting as he saw the DC-3's cargo door starting to close. "Wait! Wait! Don't leave!"

Then Rourke could see Natalia, just ahead of him, her dark hair plastered to the sides of her head, sprinting across the field, waving her arms toward the plane.

The plane was already taxiing, but as Natalia ran toward it, blocking its take-off path with her body, the plane suddenly stopped.

In a moment, Rourke was beside the fuselage, the cargo door opening, hands reaching down from inside as he handed up the old woman. He thought he heard her whisper, "God bless you, son."

Rourke turned around, seeing the white-haired old man with the AK-47, and beside him one of the Cuban

213

guards, the two of them struggling an old woman aboard the aircraft. Natalia helped an old man clamber aboard.

Rourke looked back to the plane. "Not enough room!" the crewman in the cargo door was shouting. "I can't take four of you—too much weight!"

Rourke started to turn around, his eyes meeting Natalia's. She nodded.

Thoughts raced through Rourke's mind—Sarah, the children. If he died, what would become of them? Then he looked beyond Natalia. "The damned plane over there! The Beechcraft! Come on!"

He started away from the plane. The white-haired man who'd carried the AK-47 and his wife were alone with Rourke and Natalia on the runway. Rourke had wanted it to be one of the Cuban guards, perhaps the Cuban officer. He started to shout something to the old man, but the man said, "It's all right."

Rourke started to shout, "No!" He stood there, then signaled to the crewman in the door of the DC-3. "Come on!" he shouted to Natalia, to the old man and his wife. Rourke was already running across the field toward the Beechcraft.

Rourke shouted behind him, "I'll get to the plane first—stop them! Natalia, stay with them," and Rourke bent low, the rain pouring down on him as he went into a dead run toward the small plane at the far side of the runway.

The plane was taxiing, but Rourke couldn't be certain if it was just jockeying around the field or readying for take-off again. "Wait!" Rourke shouted. "Wait!"

Rourke kept running, snatching at the twin Detonics

pistols rammed into his belt.

The ground was shaking so violently he could hardly move without falling; the cracks in the runway were widening. The plane was moving along the runway—away from him. Rourke raised both pistols into the rain-filled air and started firing them.

One shot, then another, then another, then two more. The plane wasn't slowing. Rourke kept firing. Another shot, then two rounds, then two more. He lost count, the one gun coming up empty, then the second pistol. But the plane was stopping.

Rourke jammed the guns, the actions still locked back, into his belt, then tried running faster toward the plane. The passenger door over the starboard wing opened. Rourke almost collapsed in relief. "Paul! Paul!"

He could see Rubenstein, climbing down from the wing, running across the field toward him. As the two men met, Rourke sank forward, Rubenstein's outstretched arms catching at him.

"John! Thank God it's you!"

"Paul—what the hell are you doing here?"

"My parents, John—I've gotta find them."

"I was going to stay and look for you," Rourke said. "Try," he said as he swallowed hard, getting his breath, "try somehow to get the plane to set me down near St. Petersburg if it's still there."

"I don't think it is. My parents, though—they're here, I think."

"They may have gotten out already," Rourke gasped.

"I've gotta know, John!"

Rourke just nodded, getting to his feet again. "I must

get Natalia and an older man and his wife out. Use your plane."

"What?"

"There!" and Rourke pointed behind him.

The ground was starting to break up now, the runway buckling in huge chunks. Paul Rubenstein didn't say anything. He started to run across the airfield, jumping the cracks, toward Natalia and the white-haired man and his wife. Rourke stood there, the rain pouring down on him, the wind rising so that he could barely stand erect against it.

Then Rourke started to run. Twenty-five yards ahead of him, he watched as Paul Rubenstein swept the older woman into his arms, kissing her, watched as the white-haired man hugged Rubenstein. Rourke watched as Natalia stepped back; then a smile came to her lips.

Rourke stopped running. "Jesus," he whispered. Somehow, out of all the refugees, the old man with the full shock of white hair and the woman with him were Paul Rubenstein's mother and father. Suddenly, Natalia was there, standing on her toes beside him, her lips close to his ear. "John, I understand what is driving you, now—I do." And she kissed Rourke's cheek.

Rourke looked down at the Russian girl, then shouted across the field, "Come on Paul!"

Rourke grabbed Natalia's hand, then started toward the Beechcraft, reaching the open doorway, clambering up into the plane, bypassing the pilot. He spotted Rubenstein's motorcycle and whipped out his knife, cutting away the gear strapped to it. He rolled it toward the door. He shouted out to Paul, "Get you a new one, buddy. Never take the weight."

216

"Right!" Rubenstein helped Rourke offload the bike.

In moments, Natalia had gotten Paul's mother and father aboard the plane. Rubenstein himself was the last to board.

Rourke shouted to the pilot, "Get this thing going!"

"We'll never get out of here," the pilot shouted.

Rourke climbed forward, looking over the man's shoulder. The runway was starting to split down the middle, the rain pouring down more heavily, the wind sock over the control tower spinning maddeningly. The ground was shaking beneath the plane. At the far edge of the field, Rourke could see a wall of water rising as a huge section of runway slipped across the beach area into the ocean.

"Bullshit!"

Rourke shoved the pilot out of the way and slipped behind the controls," Paul, get in there as co-pilot!"

"I can't fly."

"I'll teach you—you'll love it!" Rourke shouted, throttling up the portside engine, then the starboard. Rourke touched his fingers to his lips, then to the control wheel.

"Hang on! Here we go."

Rourke started the plane across what was left of the runway, zigzagging despite the wind, trying to find a space clear enough of the massive, ever-widening cracks for a take-off.

"All right, now or never!" Rourke shouted. To his right beyond the tip of the starboard wing, there was a massive wall of water rising, the entire airfield starting to come apart and fall into the ocean.

Rourke throttled out and the plane lurched ahead, pumping over a crack in the runway, settling down on the runway surface again. Rourke glanced to his right. The water was rushing toward them, the runway half submerged, waves starting to slosh in front of the aircraft. "Now!" Rourke shouted, pulling up, throttling out, the plane rising unsteadily. The runway and the water now roared across it as it dropped off below them.

The control tower loomed up ahead and Rourke fought the controls, working the ailerons, trying to bank the plane to starboard to miss the control tower with the portside wing tip. "Pray!" Rourke shouted, feeling Natalia's hand on his thigh as he cut the controls, seeing the control tower drop off to his left, the building already starting to collapse.

As Rourke leveled off the twin Beechcraft, he looked down. Where there had seconds before been an airport runway, now there was ocean, waves surging as far as he could see.

Chapter 49

Sarah Rourke skidded the car to a halt. The brakes were bad, she thought, but at least it had gotten her to the beach. She could see the fisherman start toward her with the children from the rocks by the beach as she exited the car.

She ran across the rain-flooded highway, dropping to her knees in the water, hugging Michael and Annie to her.

She looked up at the fisherman. "Thank you. I just couldn't have gone back with them."

"I know, lady. That Kleinschmidt is a good fella, but comes on heavy. Hey—"

What was it, she thought. "I don't understand."

"Your name Sarah?"

"Yes, I thought you—" but she stopped. She'd sent the children down with Mary Beth, had never seen the fisherman from less than a distance of several hundred feet.

"I just put it together—you and them kids. Sarah and Michael and Annie, he said."

"Who?" Sarah started up to her feet, pushing the wet hair back from her eyes.

"He's gone now. Went to Texas there by the Louisiana border to U.S. II headquarters. Some kind of mission. Name of John Rourke. Was lookin' for you."

Sarah dropped back to her knees in the rain-flooded highway, hugging her wet children to her. "Daddy's alive!" John, she thought. John . . .

She could tell the difference. Now not only was there rain water running down her cheeks, but tears.

Sarah Rourke looked up at the fisherman. "After I get the horses, how far is it?"

"I don't follow you, lady."

"To Texas, I mean." She hugged Michael and Annie again, not hearing if he had answered her or not.

Chapter 50

John Rourke stood in the rain. He'd landed the Beechcraft because the plane had almost been out of fuel. As
best he'd been able to judge from the maps, the plane
was about twenty-five miles from Chambers and U.S.
II headquarters.

Paul was sitting in the plane, talking to his parents,
the pilot had gone to find some kind of transportation.
The radio wasn't working well, too much static.

Beside Rourke stood Major Natalia Tiemerovna.
"The truce will be over soon, John—it is over now, I
think."

"At least it showed we're still human beings, didn't
it?" Rourke said quietly, his left hand cupped over his
dark tobacco cigar, his right arm around Natalia.

"You will go on looking?" she asked.

"Yes."

"Where do you plan to go?"

"The Carolinas, maybe Georgia by Savannah. She

221

was likely headed that way."

"I hope you find her—and the children."

Rourke looked at the Russian woman. Rainwater streamed down her face—and his. "Thank you, Natalia."

The woman smiled, then lowered her eyes. She stood beside Rourke in the pouring down rain.

Book Tokens

Give them
the pleasure of choosing

Book Tokens can be bought
and exchanged at most
bookshops in Great Britain
and Ireland.

THE SURVIVALIST SERIES
by Jerry Ahern